THE SHERLOCK EFFECT

THE SHERLOCK EFFECT

RAYMOND KAY LYON

THISTLE
PUBLISHING

First published in 1997 by Alibi Books

This edition published in 2017 by:

Thistle Publishing
36 Great Smith Street
London
SW1P 3BU

www.thistlepublishing.co.uk

To Marco and Shelly,
for their support and advice.

CONTENTS

ORIGINS

My father, the late Reverend Allen Webster, was a conscientious man who tended his flock with good-humoured devotion. But he had long been obsessed with Sherlock Holmes, a monomania which had a renown throughout the parish, and even beyond. The moment that was to define my life came one week before I even entered the world.

'If we are blessed with a boy,' my father remarked, as he prepared for Matins, 'I'd like to call him Sherlock. I know – it's rather unusual. But must we always be slaves to convention?'

Mother, who was generously endowed with common sense, would normally have quashed such a notion with a single withering look, but I believe she was suffering from a bad head cold at the time. She remonstrated, but only enough to force a rather messy compromise. In due course I became known, in the eyes of God and man alike, as Christopher Sherlock Webster. Can you imagine a more misconceived tribute to Conan Doyle's creation? Shortly after my sixth birthday Dad called me into his study and showed me around his collection of books and memorabilia. Here was a pipe – the very one used by William Gillette during a 1900 performance of *Sherlock Holmes* at the Garrick Theatre in New York. And over there, an edition of *The Strand* magazine from 1891.

'You're a very special fellow,' he said, in a conspiratorial tone, his portly frame looming over me. 'Do you know why?' I shook my head, wide-eyed.

'Because you have the same name as the most famous detective in the world! How about that?'

As I recall, this did not seem a particularly impressive fact at the time. Only later, when my secret got out at school, did I begin to appreciate just how special I was.

At first there was curiosity amongst my peers. But this soon degenerated into taunting and bullying. It became so unbearable that I was forced to play the comic detective, simply as a way to survive. I would stalk the playground with a magnifying glass, searching for non-existent clues. The memory still induces a *frisson*, even to this day.

And of course, my education went west.

'Do you know what's wrong with the boy?' my father would enquire vaguely, as he glanced over yet another indifferent end-of-term report. Mother would shrug, and ask me if I was happy at school. Of course, I would lie – it being the lot of children to suffer their agonies stoically and silently.

However, whenever father offered to read me any of his beloved Holmes stories I would always decline – politely, but firmly. It was, I suppose, some kind of retaliation for having been so thoughtlessly burdened at the font. And it stung him.

'Wait until he's a little older,' my mother would say. 'He'll come round in the end.'

But the older I got the more emphatic my refusals became. Dad finally gave up on me in disgust, when I was about fifteen. Our relationship broke down completely at that point, and never recovered. Two years later he died – of an undiagnosed heart condition.

Despite all these traumas I managed to secure a place at University College London to read philosophy. The course was, as I had hoped, amenable to the considered bluff – and bluff I unstintingly did.

It was in a moment of characteristic idleness during my final year that I happened to pick up a *Complete Sherlock Holmes* in paperback. For the first time ever I forwent my prejudice and began to sample those atmospheric stories. It was a strangely cathartic experience, allowing me, in a strange way, to mourn my father – something I had hitherto been quite incapable of doing.

Before very long I was a fully-fledged addict, working my way through the entire Holmes canon in a matter of weeks. After the finals I went home and made good use of the old man's collection, which, notwithstanding our differences, he had willed to me. Mother was bemused by this miraculous *volte-face*. She called it my 'Damascene conversion', with more than a hint of irony.

It certainly seemed as if Fate was dragging me, inexorably, towards that austere inhabitant of 221b...

Recent History

Allow me, gentle reader, to bring this little autobiographical narrative forward ten years – to last summer, in fact. You will excuse my glossing over the abortive foray into pop music, the failed relationships with incompatible females, and the undistinguished employment record, which characterised that intervening decade.

I was lounging in my cramped, stuffy Tufnell Park flat, entertaining nebulous ideas about careers, when the phone rang. It was none other than Morris Rennie, my old college pal.

'Mo! A voice from the past! How the devil are you?'

'I've got a little proposition for you,' he declared, in that familiar nasal tone. 'One of my uncles died last month. He's left me just over thirty grand.'

'Really?'

'Yes.'

'So, what's the proposition?'

'You remember we used to talk about setting up an agency, that handled Holmes-type problems?'

'Of course I remember.'

'Are you still into that stuff?'

'Very much so. In fact I now claim to be something of an authority on certain aspects of the subject.'

'What P.R. benefits?'

'We'll be getting the media involved eventually.'

I wasn't at all happy about that idea. 'Publicity is counter-productive for our work. But I have to admit, you've done pretty well – the effect is striking. One half expects Mrs. Hudson to potter in with a tea tray.'

'Exactly. It's all about *image*, this business.'

'Really? How would you know?'

'All business is the same,' came the glib reply. 'We must establish our market niche as early as possible.'

'More corporate-speak! That's fine, Mo, as long as you understand that deduction is an intellectual pursuit.'

'Someone has to think about the bottom line,' he insisted. 'There aren't any more rich uncles to fall back on, you know.'

My friend paced the room, his lanky, besuited frame bent forward almost to defy gravity. The expression on that long, narrow face was sour.

To avert a row I conceded that presentation was, of course, quite important. 'But there are limits. For example, you wouldn't want me to prance around in Victorian clothes, would you?'

His frown dissolved into an impish grin. 'You've been reading my mind again, Sherl. Have a look in that trunk, would you?'

I lifted the lid and my worst fears were realized. Here was a complete wardrobe of Holmesian attire – frock-coat, deerstalker, smoking jacket etc.

'Oh no you don't!' I cried. 'You'll never catch me in these!'

'Just think about it for a moment. People will flock from around the world for a consultation. It's a marketing man's dream!'

'In case you haven't noticed,' I remarked, firmly closing up the chest, 'I'm five foot eight, several pounds overweight, and I'm certainly not blessed with aquiline features. How do we get round that? A crash diet? Plastic surgery? No, perhaps you'd better not answer that at the moment.'

By the end of the week we had, miraculously, agreed upon the following draft of an advertisement, which was duly dispatched to the broadsheet newspapers:

THE BASKERVILLE AGENCY
Will Investigate All Mysterious and Bizarre
Occurences
Apply in confidence to:
Christopher Sherlock Webster Esq.,
237 Crawford St., off Baker St., London W.1.
www.thebaskervilleagency.co.uk

Let it be recorded that I was opposed to the inclusion of my middle name, simply on the grounds that it would seem gimmicky. Mo was adamant, however. He ranted on about the need for 'strong branding' and had the gall to say it was a 'resignation issue' for him. In the end I acquiesced, just as I knew I must on the sartorial issue. It might sound craven to you, but money tends to talk in these situations.

All we could do now was sit back, like a couple of weekend anglers, and await the first gentle tug on the line ...

Early public reaction was far from auspicious. I fielded a steady trickle of telephone enquiries, none of which led to anything. Many believed the advertisement was a hoax, and complimented me on my sense of humour. Others expected to be offered some kind of ghastly Holmes-a-gram service to enliven their office parties. One old fool was even convinced I was recruiting for a mystical cult, and became extremely abusive when I denied it.

However, hidden amongst all this chaff appeared such a grain of wheat as we had no right to expect so soon. The case in question is presented for your delectation in the following pages, along with four others.

If I have tended to dwell upon my successes rather than my failures it is not out of egoism; rather an urge to demonstrate what may still be achieved through the uncompromising application of deductive logic.

THE FUR TRADE

CHAPTER ONE

'My name is Byron Silk,' began the caller, speaking with a decided West Indian modulation.

'How can I be of service?' I replied urbanely.

'I'm Vicki Vine's personal assistant.'

'Vicki Vine? You don't mean the soul chanteuse?'

'That's right, the singer. She's in a lot of trouble.'

'I'm sorry to hear that,' I commiserated. 'Perhaps we could set up a consultation for her? I'm free most of this week.'

'She'll send the limo round to your place,' said the man peremptorily. 'Six thirty this evening.'

'Alright. But couldn't you give me something more to go on, Mr. Silk? I like to know roughly what I'm getting into.'

'It may be a matter of life and death,' he confided darkly.

'Indeed? Is she in some kind of physical danger?'

'Can't say anything more on the phone.'

'Very well. Tell her I'll be ready at half past six.'

The caller hung up, leaving me to consider whether he might in fact be some kind of crank. I decided it was unlikely.

Mo dropped in about an hour later, and was understandably thrilled at the prospect of having a pop star as a client.

'Let's think about your clothes,' he said, clucking round me like an old hen. 'How about top-hat, frock-coat, pearl-grey trousers?'

'If you insist.'

'Try to butter her up a bit,' he advised, pulling the items out of the costume-chest. 'Massage her ego. Tell her she's the best thing since Aretha Franklin. You can do that, can't you?'

'Perhaps,' I replied non-committally, '*if* we decide to take the case on. It must depend on certain factors.'

Mo looked outraged. 'What do you mean? What factors?'

'I mean her problem must be susceptible to those very methods of deductive analysis which we have been at pains to advertise.'

'You're having me on!'

'I'm deadly serious. We must stick to our speciality – the bizarre, the recondite, the subtle. Otherwise the whole project is doomed from the outset. I'm sorry to be purist about this, Morris.'

'Look, Sherl,' said Mo, putting a hand on my shoulder matily, 'we can't afford to throw away a high-profile client like Vicki Vine. She could be the making of us. Just find out what kind of trouble she's in, then tell her we'll sort it out. If she needs protection we'll hire some muscle.'

I snorted my disgust. This was all beginning to sound too much like an episode of *Minder*.

'Unfortunately I'll have to leave in about half an hour,' he added, glancing at his watch.

'So you won't be here when she arrives?'

'Sorry. I've got this crucial meeting with my old business partner. We're winding up the company, and I have to make sure it's done properly. You'll have to handle this on your own, I'm afraid.'

✤ ✤ ✤

As I sat alone in our Victorian theme parlour, surveying the desultory comings and goings of Crawford Street, I slowly began to come round to Mo's way of thinking.

'There's money in this case, Watson, if there is nothing else,' Holmes had once remarked, upon seeing a brougham and pair draw up outside. Even the great man, then, was not above occasional venality. In any case, Vicki Vine could well be said to be an 'illustrious client' in the modern context. She might even provide an entrée into the entertainment aristocracy.

I walked over to the full-length mirror and inspected my dated attire. Although everything fitted remarkably well I still felt like a second-rate provincial actor who was struggling to grow into a new role.

Over a hastily prepared tea, I scoured my Book of Hit Singles. It appeared that Vicki Vine's recording career was even more illustrious than I had realized. There had been five top-twenty singles; including the well-remembered Blood Is Thicker Than Water, which peaked at number 5 in 2012. I rang her record company, Cresta, and learned from a helpful publicist that Vine had made lucrative inroads into the European and U.S. markets. Her first album had gone silver in the States. She'd enjoyed sales in excess of ten million units throughout the world. But as to her exact earnings to date my informant was understandably coy, preferring to say that Vicki need never 'vocalise' again.

Having armed myself with this background knowledge I could do little else but sit, in costume, and make idle speculations as to the nature of the singer's predicament.

Eventually, two impatient hoots caused me to peer out through our genteel lace curtains. A maroon Jag XF with tinted windows had double-parked directly opposite.

As no-one emerged from the vehicle I assumed that I was being summoned. I grabbed my topper, swallowed hard, and hurried out into the fierce July sun. My anachronistic appearance elicited amused and even worried stares from the public – but I strode manfully on towards the waiting limousine. The rear door opened. I slid in, and found myself shoulder-to-shoulder with one of Britain's most successful black artistes.

Not that one could have sworn it was her, at first. She wore impenetrable dark glasses, and her head was swathed in a red scarf. I mumbled an introduction and presented one of our newly-printed business cards.

'Baskerville's. That sounds good,' she said abstractedly, as we cruised off.

'Your assistant, Mr. Silk, implied that you might be in some danger. Perhaps if you could give me a clear account of–'

Before I could complete my well-rehearsed request Miss Vine threw a CD into my lap, entitled *Class*. It was one of her own. The photograph on the front certainly caught the eye; she was depicted naked, languishing on a chaise-longue, bedecked in pearls and a tiara, her modesty preserved only by strategically draped fur stoles. I recognized an ermine piece, a leopardskin, and what appeared to be Persian lamb. Her hair was blown away from her face by a wind-machine, Diana Ross-style, and the glossy lips curled into an enigmatic smile.

'Extremely decorative,' I said, somewhat abashed. 'The furs look splendid.'

'That picture has caused me a lot of hassle,' Vicki declared ruefully. 'By the way, are you any good at kidnaps?'

'Kidnaps? You mean carrying them out?'

'No, I mean investigating them.'

'Yes,' I bluffed. 'Actually, that's what I specialize in.'

'Good.'

We stopped at some traffic lights. I sensed that she was looking me over, which made me feel rather uncomfortable. 'Do you normally dress like this?' she asked at last.

'This? Oh, it goes with the job,' I replied, with a silly laugh.

She picked up my lustrous top-hat from the seat and began to finger it admiringly. I was afraid she was about to enquire *how long I'd been in the detection business,* so I quickly returned to the matter in hand.

'What, exactly, do you want me to do, Miss Vine?'

She sighed. 'It's Jake, my boyfriend. He's been kidnapped by animal rights people. They're real nutters – you know – extremists.'

'I see. When did this happen?'

'Three days ago. It's not the first time, either.'

'Really?'

'Same thing happened about a month ago. They sent me a ransom demand. I paid up, and we got Jake back safely.'

'What was the sum involved, if I may ask?'

'Two hundred thousand pounds.'

'That much?' I said, giving a low whistle. 'And you never informed the police?'

Vicki shook her head. 'I thought if I paid up without a fuss they wouldn't bother us again. But it hasn't worked out like that.'

I took out a notebook and pen from the pocket of my frock-coat. 'Do you mind if I jot down a few things?'

'If you want.'

'Your boyfriend's name, again, is?'

'Jake Humber. Like the river.'

'Or the car,' I added lightly. There was no reaction – perhaps she was too young to remember. 'What does he do for a living?'

'Music journalist. Freelance.'

'Why do you think he was targeted by the animal rights group?'

'He was my boyfriend, and I was their public enemy number one.'

'Just because you posed in furs?'

'That's right. There was a big campaign against me in the press when the CD came out – don't you remember? "Pop Star in Fur Scandal", "Vicki Vine Accused of Animal Cruelty", that sort of thing.'

'Yes, I do recollect something of the kind.'

'They kidnapped Jake because he was easy to get at. I had security people around me. But the stupid thing is those furs were fake – all of them.'

'Are you quite sure?' I asked, with a sceptical look.

Vicki removed her dark glasses for emphasis. 'Yes, I'm sure. I love animals. I don't think I've ever worn genuine fur. Not deliberately, anyway.'

'How do you explain the press stories, then?'

She shrugged. 'They got their facts wrong – as usual. And I got a sackful of hate mail. Even obscene phone calls. But nothing serious happened, until the first kidnap.'

'Have you kept that ransom letter?'

'I thought you'd want to see it,' she replied, producing a large manilla envelope from her hip pocket. It was addressed;

Ms. V. Vine, 38 Heath View Avenue, Hampstead,
London N.W.6
URGENT AND CONFIDENTIAL

The postmark was Hastings. Inside was a single sheet of paper bearing the following chilling message;

Dear Vicki,

We have Jake Humber. The price for his safe return is £200,000.

This Sunday (June 12th), at precisely 12.00 midnight, put the cash into a briefcase and deposit in the dustbin outside No. 12, Dock End Lane, Brixton. Come alone, and leave the vicinity directly afterwards. We will let you know where to collect Jake once we have the money.

If you fail to pay, or involve the police, we will kill Jake immediately. His blood will be on your hands, just like those defenceless animals butchered to satisfy your vanity.

Please find enclosed fur, and photo. Remember our spies are everywhere!

Thanking you in anticipation of your generous contribution,

A.D.M. (Animal Defence Militia).

P.S. Why not keep the fur in that pretty little Japanese vase in your bedroom?

Paper-clipped to the letter was a photograph, showing a thin, pale, frightened young man, standing in a featureless room. He wore only underpants, and was handcuffed and blindfolded.

'What did they mean by "fur"?' I enquired.

'There was a lock of Jake's hair in the envelope. It's their little joke.'

'I see. Tell me more about that Sunday. You drove alone to Brixton?'

'Byron Silk came with me, but when we got near Dock End Lane I dropped him off. I put the money in the dustbin, like they told me. There was a note stuck on the lid, saying "Go to phone box in Beacon Road, Paignton, Devon for next instructions."'

'Quite a journey!' I exclaimed.

'Yes, but I had to go. Byron did most of the driving. When we got there we found another note, telling us to find a bus-shelter outside The Freemasons Arms, in Northampton.'

'How long did that take you?'

'We never actually went there. I phoned the pub instead, and asked them to help me. I said we were doing a T.V. game show. The landlord was very helpful. He went to the bus stop and read the message over the phone.'

'That was very resourceful!' I laughed.

'It was Byron's idea.'

'So, what was the next message?'

'We had to go to an empty cottage in Sussex, called the Bird's Nest. And that's where we found Jake. He was locked up in one of the bedrooms.'

'Could he describe the kidnappers?' I asked hopefully.

'He was blindfolded all the time. But there were definitely three of them; one bossy guy with a Scottish accent who did most of the talking, a girl, and another guy. They called the Scottish one "Mac". Not much of a clue, is it?'

'No,' I agreed. 'How did they treat him?'

'One meal a day. Crap food. And they never let him out of the bedroom. Not once.'

'Was he surprised when you turned up?'

'No. They'd told him the ransom had been paid, and someone would collect him soon.'

'One more thing,' I said, turning the page of my note-book. 'Did Jake describe how he was kidnapped?'

'He couldn't remember anything – he was on a bender at the time.'

'Drink?'

'Yes. Jake has a problem, to put it politely,' admitted Vicki in a long-suffering tone. 'The first thing he remembers is waking up in a strange room with handcuffs on.'

'Good,' I said, drawing a line under my notes, 'that puts me in the picture regarding the first kidnap. Now, tell me all about the latest abduction.'

'Alright. But let's get some fresh air first,' she suggested, stretching her limbs.

Throughout the interview we had been cruising around central London quite aimlessly, and now Green Park had opened up on our left. Vine leant forward and tapped the chauffeur on the shoulder.

'Could you stop here, please,' she instructed. 'We won't be long – about half an hour. Grab a sandwich if you like.'

Our liveried driver grunted something inaudible and pulled up. Once we had alighted the Jag purred off down Piccadilly in search of a parking space.

'That's a hired car, you know,' Vicki remarked. 'I normally drive an Aston Martin.'

'Why the switch?'

'So *they* don't see me talking to you, of course! I've got to be careful.'

We found a bench shaded by plane trees and sat down, drinking in the sun-baked scenery for a while. Vicki removed her head-scarf and dark glasses; I noticed a hunted, fearful look in her eyes. Her face was drawn with fatigue, and to be honest she no more than approximated her glamorous public image.

'You've left your top-hat in the car,' she observed, with a note of disappointment.

'Yes, I didn't like to be too conspicuous, given the delicate circumstances.'

'By the way, are you really Sherlock, or is that a kind of stage name?'

I smiled. 'No, it's my official middle name.'

'Do you want me to call you that?'

I pondered for a while. 'How about Sherl? It's a nickname my colleague uses.'

'Sherl,' she repeated to herself. 'Yes, that's cool. My real name is Sally Jones. Boring, isn't it? I prefer Vicki.'

I drew out my notebook again. 'Well, Vicki, if you're ready, we ought to move on to the second kidnap. You said it occurred only three days ago?'

'Yes. Jake was just beginning to get over the first one. It had shaken him up pretty badly. This time they grabbed him outside the restaurant where we were eating. I couldn't believe it!'

'Can you give me more details?' I requested.

'Well, it was a surprise meal that Jake had organised for me. His way of thanking me – for saving his life!'

'By paying the original ransom, you mean?'

'Yes. I didn't want him to feel grateful. But he insisted.' She looked at me intently. 'When someone you care about is in danger money doesn't mean anything, does it? I would have paid twice as much if it was necessary – I told him that.'

'Which restaurant did you go to?'

'Fosca's. It's a little Italian place on the King's Road. He booked us the best table, by the window. When we'd finished our dessert I wanted a cigarette, but we'd both run out. He said he'd pop out to the car and get another packet. After about twenty minutes I started to worry, because there was no sign of him.'

A shadow of distress passed over the singer's features. Obviously these moments of her story were painful to relate. 'I looked out of the window, and there he was. In the back seat of a strange car. It was going right past the restaurant – slowly – that's why I noticed it. Jake was trying to say something to me through the car window. He was struggling, his hands were tied behind his back. I'll never forget that look on his face – not fear, exactly – more surprise. As if he was thinking; how can this be happening to me again? It was terrible ... '

'Who was driving the car?'

'A man. I only got a glimpse. He had grey hair, I think. Ordinary face. He was grinning.'

'Would you recognise him again?'

'I'm not sure.'

'No-one else in the car?'

'Not that I could see.'

'What was the make?'

'Could've been an Audi, B.M.W., something like that. Dark colour.'

'Number plate?'

'I ran into the street to see, but it was too far away. Then I phoned Sandy O'Neill, my manager, from the restaurant. She told me to go straight over to her place – which I did. Sandy's brilliant in a crisis. She's a good mate, as well as a manager.'

'And have you received another ransom note yet?'

Vicki nodded. 'This morning. Left it in the Jag, I'm afraid.' She sighed. 'But it's not very interesting anyway.'

'Not interesting? How do you mean?'

'It's the same as before, except now they're asking for £500,000.'

'You mean they simply typed in a different figure?'

'That's it. Oh, and the deadline is next Sunday.'

'Audacious,' I muttered, 'extremely audacious.'

We sat in silence, both oppressed by the gravity of the situation.

'I think you should seriously consider going to the police this time,' I said at last. 'Of course, I'm willing to help in any way I can. But, frankly, they have more resources at their disposal.'

'How can I risk it?' she wailed despairingly. 'You've seen the threats – those bastards are everywhere. Anyway, you said you could handle kidnaps.'

'I'm only thinking of your best interests,' I replied reasonably.

She got up from the bench with a determined expression. 'I'll just have to get Jake back on my own then. I never wanted to call you in the first place. It was all Sandy's idea.'

With that she stomped off across the park.

I hurried after her, picturing how Mo would react to my losing the commission. 'Hang on! I didn't say I wouldn't take your case. I just want you to consider all the options first.'

'Make up your mind,' she snapped, swinging round.

'Clearly you can't keep paying off these criminals, Vicki. Next time they'll ask for a million, then five million. Where will it all end? Do you really love Jake enough to bankrupt yourself?'

She gave a slightly defensive pout at that remark. 'I've told you how much I care for him.' Then her expression softened. 'Sandy's right, though. I can't handle this on my own any more. It's destroying me.'

'Alright,' I said in a decisive tone, 'if you give me a free hand I'll see what I can do. It should be possible to discover more about the method and character of the kidnappers. Are they likely to bluff? Have they ever kidnapped anyone else? If so, what was the outcome? All that would be a start, at least.'

'We'll have to be very, very careful,' she warned, in a low voice.

'Of course. Perhaps I'd better stick to modern dress from now on, even if it means incurring the wrath of my partner.'

Suitably assured, Vicki led the way back to the waiting limousine and our morose driver.

'Crawford Street,' she ordered, settling down into the back seat.

There was a grunt of assent, then we started off.

The conversation turned to Vicki's career. For the first time that day the singer began to look relaxed, ebullient even. She spoke of how the new album was going. There were even a couple of funny anecdotes, and a whit of gossip about a promiscuous record producer.

'What's wrong, Sherl?' she asked, when I failed to respond to her last joke. 'You look worried.'

'It's probably nothing,' I replied, as casually as I could, 'but that red B.M.W. seems to have been following us since Green Park. Could it be the same one you saw outside the Italian restaurant?'

'Y-es, I suppose so. That's a woman driving, isn't it?'

Our pursuer had very frizzy blond hair in a rather seventies style. She wore dark glasses, and a wide-brimmed hat that would have graced any Royal Ascot day. I made a note of the registration number.

'Didn't Jake say one of the kidnappers was a woman?' I asked.

'That's right.'

'Well, there's only one way to find out for sure.' I leant forward to address the chauffeur. 'Carry on up Gloucester Place till you get to Regent's Park, then drive all the way round it.'

'Thought you wanted Crawford Street?' he objected gruffly.

'Just do it!' shouted Vicki.

The B.M.W. followed us slavishly in a complete circle back to the Marylebone Road, maintaining a respectful distance.

'Mm. That can't possibly be a coincidence.'

'What do we do?' asked Vicki, unconsciously clinging at the sleeve of my frock-coat.

'There's nothing to do. If we stop to confront her she'll simply drive off and alert the gang – with unpredictable consequences.'

'You mean Jake would be in danger?'

'It's not worth the risk. As it is, she has no reason to think I'm a detective.'

'You'd better be right.'

'There's no cause for alarm,' I soothed, in a tone which hardly reflected my real concern. 'Now, I recommend that we take a sudden turn to the left, and left again. I'll jump out and disappear – into the nearest shop or pub. You then make your way home using the most eccentric route possible.'

'When do we meet again?'

'Tomorrow. I'd like you to show me round your house.'

'Are you mad! They'll be watching it – constantly.'

'We'll have to work something out, then. Are you at home tomorrow?'

'I'm in the recording studio till seven in the evening. It would have to be after eight.'

'Expect me around eight thirty, then.'

CHAPTER TWO

That evening I updated Morris on the phone. We arranged to convene at the office at half past nine· the following morning.

When I arrived my colleague was on his knees just inside the front door, with his ear pressed to a large package.

'What the hell are you doing?' I asked, standing over him.

'I thought I heard ticking,' he explained, looking up at me with wild eyes. 'You have a listen – but don't move it, for Christ's sake!'

I could hear nothing but the rushing of my own blood. 'You must have imagined it, Mo,' I concluded, getting to my feet. 'Anyway, this parcel isn't even addressed to us – it's for the travel agents on the top floor.'

'It could still blow up the whole building,' he insisted, scrutinising the other mail with equal intensity. 'I've already gone through those rubbish bags. They're OK.'

I managed to tear Mo away from his security check, and we climbed the stairs to our own floor.

'Examine the door,' he advised, as I got out my key. 'They may have booby-trapped the lock.'

'This thing has really got to you, hasn't it?' I remarked, as we safely entered our apartment.

'If there's one thing I can't handle it's terrorism,' pronounced Mo bitterly, searching each room in turn for explosive devices.

In the end he seemed reasonably satisfied, and sat down on the sofa with a blow of the cheeks. The weather was exceptionally humid, and trickles of sweat were already beginning to make their way down his bullet-shaped head.

'You may think I'm over-reacting,' he said, fanning his face with a magazine, 'but if these animal rights loonies were following you they probably know exactly where we work by now.'

'It's possible,' I conceded, opening a window to encourage a draught. 'But I don't see why they would target us, necessarily.'

'At least you can't complain that it's a dull case.'

'On the contrary,' I retorted, 'stripped of the sensationalism which attends pop stars, terrorists, and large sums of money, it struggles to rise above the banal. However, we press on. Vicki's manager will be here shortly. I rang her yesterday; she seemed most anxious to assist us. You never know – she might even add another layer of complexity.'

Mo put the hoover over the carpet and I dusted the furniture, in honour of our first official visitor.

Sandy O'Neill arrived somewhat earlier than the appointed hour, carrying a briefcase, and looking generally very business-like. She was in her early forties, with pleasing, definite features, and a shiny, manageable bob.

'Very good of you to see us at short notice, Miss O'Neill,' I remarked, pouring her a cup of coffee from our handsome service. 'I know how busy you are. You manage several other artists apart from Vicki, or am I misinformed?'

'She takes up most of my time, of course,' answered Sandy with a quick smile, 'especially with the new album being launched soon.'

'It was you who advised her to contact us, I understand? No doubt you spotted our little advertisement?'

'That's right. To be brutally honest, Mr. Webster, I would have preferred Vicki to go straight to the police. But she refused point-blank.'

'Well, I'm gratified you chose us as your second option.'

'Shall we get down to the nitty gritty?' suggested our guest solemnly. 'What are we going to do about Jake? Do we pay off the kidnappers – again – or what?'

'We have a few days in which to make that decision,' I replied evenly, 'which is really why I asked you to come and see us, Miss O'Neill. Any information you can provide will be appreciated.'

She shrugged. 'Ask me whatever you want.'

'Let's start at the beginning, then. Can you remember whose idea it was to photograph Vicki wearing only fur stoles?'

'Mine, I'm afraid. I thought a kind of "rich bitch" image would really sell the album; Vicki agreed. Obviously, if I'd known the press would twist everything and make out the furs were genuine, I'd never have suggested it.'

'So, you're absolutely certain the furs were artificial?'

'Of course! I particularly wanted to avoid a reaction from the animal welfare lobby – so I asked the shop to double check when I bought them. What more could I do?'

'Is it normal for you to buy Vicki's costumes personally?'

'I do it occasionally – if she's too busy.'

'When the stories started to appear did you consider putting out a statement, assuring the public that no genuine fur had been used?'

'We did put out a statment like that. Several, actually. But the mud had already stuck.'

'I see. Couldn't you have sued the papers for libel, in that case?'

'We considered it, but there were obstacles.'

'Such as?'

'Well, for a start the "evidence" disappeared. Didn't Vicki tell you? The furs were stolen from out of her bedroom.'

'When was this?' I asked, exchanging a glance with Mo.

'Just after the media got hold of the story. I told Vicki to inform the police immediately, which she did. But they were never recovered.'

'You worry me, Miss O'Neill,' I reacted gravely. 'It begins to look more and more like some kind of conspiracy against Vicki.'

'I see what you mean,' she agreed.

'Going back to the furs,' put in Mo, 'have you kept the receipt? That would be good evidence that they were artificial.'

Sandy looked rather embarrassed. 'I lost it out of my purse, actually. Stupid of me.'

She snatched a packet of cigarettes from her handbag – her hands trembling very slightly. 'You don't mind?' she asked, before lighting up.

'Feel free,' I said.

'It's a filthy habit, I know. In fact I've been trying to give up, but it's a lot harder than meat.'

'Sorry?'

'I became a vegetarian over a year ago – stuck to it ever since. But the dreaded weed is something else.'

She let out a nervy giggle.

'Presumably, then, you think it's inherently wrong to kill animals for food?' I asked, nimbly.

'Yes, I do,' she replied instinctively, then, seeing our reaction, added: 'but I'm not militant about it, if that's what you're thinking. These extremists who use violence are no better than any other terrorists. They're scum!'

Sandy's hazel eyes hardened behind the plumes of smoke issuing from her glossy lips. Just then it was easy to imagine how she must have clawed and hussled her way to the top of the pop management pile.

'Tell me,' I said, replenishing her coffee cup with a serene smile, 'how did you first come to manage Vicki?'

'Through Jake, really – we go back years. He discovered her, did you know that?'

'No.'

'She was in an all-girl dance act that wasn't really going anywhere. Jake realized Vicki had a fantastic voice. He wrote lots of positive stuff about her in *Turntable* magazine, and on the back of that she got a solo deal with Cresta Records.'

'It's funny,' she continued reminiscently, 'because at the time he was dating one of the other girls in the group – Denise, I think her name was. Next thing we knew Jake and Vicki were an item.'

'Was Denise bitter?'

'Extremely, at first. But she's happily married with two kids now.'

'All forgiven and forgotten, you think?'

'Far as I know.'

'And what of Jake himself? How do you think he'll react under the strain of being a hostage – for a second time? You obviously know the man pretty well.'

'All I know is that he's been rather fragile for some time now,' confided Sandy.

'You mean physically?'

'And emotionally. What with his drink and cocaine habits, and all the ups and downs with Vicki.'

'Ups and downs?'

'Well, last year they were going to get married – it was announced and everything. Then Jake's boozing got worse. Vicki forked out for him to go to the Clearwater Project – that's a residential rehab place in Somerset. All the celebs go there for drying out – actors, musos, writers.'

'I think I've heard of it,' said Mo. 'It's got a good reputation.'

'You're totally cut off from the outside world, there; no T.V., newspapers – even letters are banned. Anyway, by the time he came out Vicki had changed her mind about marrying him.'

'Why was that?' I asked.

'Her career was really starting to buzz. America was catching on to the first album. I guess she just needed time to reassess her priorities.'

'What's the latest situation between them?'

'They've come to an "understanding" – isn't that the right term? Vicki will be devoting the next five years to her career. If by the end of that time Jake has got himself under control then she'll tie the knot.'

'Sounds like an eminently reasonable arrangement,' I remarked appreciatively. 'I don't suppose you had a hand in it?'

Vicki's manager smiled demurely. 'I might have done. But it's all completely academic if we don't get Jake back in one piece.'

'As you say, Miss O'Neill, as you say... Well, I think that's all for now. Thanks very much for your time – it's been most interesting. We'll keep you informed of any developments, of course.'

I got up and showed her courteously to the door. She paused in order to cast a final, critical eye over our parlour.

'I really like the way you've done this out. Who's your designer?'

I pointed to Mo, who gave a self-mocking bow.

'If you want to earn some extra money you could always come and do my bedroom.'

'I'll bear that in mind,' he laughed.

'Oh, before I go,' said Sandy, turning to me inquisitively, 'there's something I've been meaning to ask you.'

'Let me guess, you want to know if my middle name really is Sherlock.'

She looked startled. 'How did you know what I was going to say?'

'Good old-fashioned guesswork,' I replied with a wink.

That evening, a warm and sultry one, we drove up to Hampstead. I parked my trusty Nissan on Heath View Avenue, several hundred yards away from Vicki's house, then we approached on foot.

Mindful of our client's concerns, I was disguised in a trendy jacket, baseball cap, baggy jeans, and chunky trainers. A guitar was slung rebelliously over my shoulder. Mo's appearance was similar.

The pop star's house was an imposing, turreted, neo-Gothic pile set back some way from the road. We crunched up the gravel drive under the eerie gaze of two security cameras, mounted on tree trunks.

Our ring on the doorbell brought a large, affable-looking woman to the threshold. She showed us into the living room, which was minimally furnished and predominantly white. By contrast, a black grand piano stood in the corner, upon which Vicki was strumming abstractedly.

'Your visitors, Miss Vine,' announced the woman (whom I took to be the housekeeper).

'Ah, Sherl!' reacted our famous client, looking up. 'I like the gear, by the way!'

'Thank you.'

'You weren't followed here, were you?'

'I trust not. Let me introduce my colleague, Morris Rennie.'

Mo slipped off his cap, and stepped forward with a sickly grin. 'Good to meet you at last. I really love your music.'

'Oh, thanks,' replied Vicky, rather flatly.

'Was that a new song you were working on? Sounded great,' he continued sycophantically.

'That? No way! I was just mucking about. So you're a fan, are you?'

'Definitely.'

'Which album do you like best?'

Mo froze in panic.

'It's ... er ... it's really difficult to choose, you know,' he stammered.

'I've only made two,' she pointed out frostily.

'Didn't you say you liked *Vine Vinyl*?' I put in, coming to Mo's rescue.

'That's right! If I had to choose, it would be – er – that one.'

My colleague shrank back, deflated by his *faux pas*.

'So, to business,' I said briskly. 'I take it there's been no further word from the kidnappers?'

'Nothing,' replied our client sombrely.

'In that case, may we possibly see your bedroom? There are a couple of things I need to confirm.'

Vicki shrugged, then disengaged herself from the piano, and led us upstairs into an impressive chamber, which was dominated by an exquisite four-poster bed.

'Now, where is this Japanese vase that was mentioned in the ransom note?' I asked, looking round.

'I used to have one,' she explained, 'but I sold it about six months ago. And it wasn't Japanese, it was Chinese.'

'Where did you keep it?'

'Here, on this window-sill.'

'I see. Well, whoever wrote that ransom letter was obviously acting on old and inaccurate intelligence. Can you think of any strangers who may have had access to this bedroom – at the time when the vase was still here?'

Vicki contemplated for a while. 'Loads of people, actually. I had the whole place redecorated last autumn. There were workmen coming and going all the time.'

I sighed. 'That hardly narrows the field. Of course, there is an alternative possibility; the vase may have been seen from outside...'

I went to the oriel window and calculated several lines of sight.

'Who owns that house over the road?' I asked.

'A High Court judge. Lived there for years.'

'Perhaps he's an animal lover?'

Vicki was tickled by the idea. 'He goes fox-hunting regularly.'

'Oh! Then I think we can safely rule him out. Alright, let's move on to the furs. They were stolen from this room, weren't they?'

'Yes, I kept them in here,' replied the singer, pointing to a substantial oak wardrobe in the corner.

'And did the theft take place when the decorators were in, by any chance?'

'Yes. Do you think one of them did it?'

'Entirely possible. Somebody from the A.D.M. must have been in this room – that's clear.'

Later that evening Vicki gave us an impromptu rendition of her hits on the piano, which was a most pleasant interlude. Then Byron Silk arrived unexpectedly.

Vicki's Man Friday turned out to be a lithe rastafarian with an outwardly stern manner who broke into an engaging grin upon the least occasion.

'We spoke on the phone,' he began, slapping me on the hand in the street-wise fashion. 'Any news about Jake?'

'I'm afraid not,' I answered gravely. 'But we still have four days to pay the ransom. I plan to go down to Sussex tomorrow; I'll take a look round the cottage where you found him last time.'

'The kidnappers wouldn't use the same place again, surely,' objected Mo.

'No, but they may have left some traces.'

'Would you like me to come along?' suggested Byron. 'I could show you exactly where we found Jake.'

'Good idea,' agreed Vicki. 'I can't join you, I'm afraid – there's another recording session in the afternoon.'

At that moment the housekeeper came in to announce that supper was served. We relocated to the sumptuous Regency dining-room.

The food was French, impeccably presented, and the conversation was as bright as could be expected, overshadowed as we were by poor Jake's perilous situation.

By the time Mo and I finally took our leave dusk had descended. The house loomed behind us like a Hammer movie set, and we came once again under the unblinking scrutiny of the security cameras.

'Vicki seems to be bearing up pretty well,' remarked Mo, once we had emerged into the avenue. 'A bit nervy perhaps, but you'd never guess her boyfriend was being held by terrorists.'

'She keeps herself busy,' I replied, 'which is the best kind of therapy.'

As we neared my car Mo declared: 'We really must buy you something more stylish, Sherl. A Nissan Micra hardly meets the case. Remember what I said about image.'

'At least it's reliable,' I countered. 'What would you have me go around in? A hansom?'

'Let me have a think about it.'

'You do that, Mo. You do that.'

I stood in the road, fumbling around in the gloom for my car keys.

'Look at that prat driving without lights!' exclaimed my friend, pointing up the road.

I turned to see a murky form heading towards us at a crawl. Once it was within about fifty yards it suddenly accelerated with a roar. I hardly had time to recognize the make of the car – a B.M.W. – and observe that the driver had long blonde hair, before it was virtually upon me! Everything seemed to progress in slow motion, and my feet felt as if they were rooted to the tarmac. Just one second more of inaction and I would have been mown down. Fortunately, however, something like a survival instinct clicked on in my brain. I made a desperate, goalkeeper's lunge across the Nissan's bonnet. There was a horrendous scraping noise, then the B.M.W. screamed off towards the twilit heath.

The next thing I knew Mo was bending over me anxiously. I was lying face-up on the pavement – dazed, though seemingly in tact.

'Are you OK, Sherl? I'll get an ambulance.'

I shook my head stubbornly. 'No need. I'm fine. She missed me completely.'

With some effort I managed to lever myself up onto my elbows.

'Stay absolutely still – in case something's broken.'

'Nothing's broken. I think I'd know. Just help me up, will you?'

Against his better judgement Mo pulled me, slowly, to my feet. I leant on the car roof to steady myself.

'Who the hell was that maniac anyway?' asked Mo.

'The same charming young lady who honoured us with her attentions yesterday. By the way, you saved my life. If I hadn't turned round –'

'Forget that! We should get you to a doctor, or at least back to Vicki's house; those cuts need seeing to.'

'Vicki's under enough strain as it is. Why don't you just drive me to my flat, like an excellent chap.'

Back in my sitting room Mo dabbed at my grazes with cotton wool soaked in T.C.P. During his ministrations I began to shake, quite uncontrollably.

'It's delayed shock, that's all,' he diagnosed. 'We'll have to keep you warm, though.'

'You missed your profession,' I managed to say through chattering teeth, as a blanket was draped over me.

The following morning I woke very early from a fitful, unpleasant sleep. Mo had bedded down on the sofa. I crept achingly past him into the kitchenette and made myself a pot of tea and some toast. The noise must have disturbed him because he appeared within a few seconds, rubbing the sleep from his eyes.

'How are you feeling this morning?' he yawned.

'Stiff – all over,' I replied. 'Thanks for looking after me last night, though.'

'That woman tried to kill you – no doubt about it. What have we let ourselves in for, Sherl?'

'A dangerous case,' I admitted. 'And I think we may consider ourselves well and truly warned off.'

'But you still want to carry on?'

'We can hardly throw in the towel every time there's a minor reverse.'

'Minor reverse? Look at you!'

True, I was not a particularly pretty sight, now that the bruises had blossomed into full technicolour.

'Oh well,' said Mo, lifting the teapot with a resigned air, 'I suppose if you're game, I'm game.'

'Spoken like a true Watson! A man of the right kidney.'

'Leave my internal organs out of this.'

'By the way, I'm still driving down to Sussex today, with Byron.'

'In your state?'

'I'll be alright.'

'What about me?' objected my colleague, feeding the toaster with a slice of bread and looking hurt.

'You can have a go at tracing the B.M.W., with the help of that friend on the Force that you're always mentioning. Oh, and I'd like you to contact some of the legitimate animal rights societies. See what they know about the Animal Defence Militia.'

After breakfast I headed gingerly for the bedroom to get dressed.

'We don't want any more near-misses like last night,' said Mo, watching me with a concerned frown. 'Be careful. Don't take any unnecessary risks.'

I picked up Byron Silk an hour later, from a rehearsal studio in a grim, Dickensian warehouse near London Bridge. He had just finished a practice session with his own, as yet undiscovered, band.

On the journey south we chatted, mainly about the current state of pop music. I played him some of my old stuff, he played his reggae. We crossed into smiling, undulating Sussex in good time.

The Bird's Nest was roughly equidistant between Hastings and Rye, near a tiny village called Berry Cross.

The whole area was densely wooded – so much so that we completely missed the turning, and had to double back.

A narrow, suspension-testing lane tunnelled through a wall of foliage towards the cottage. It soon deteriorated into an unpassable track; we were forced to abandoned the car and walk the rest of the way, coming at last to a garden quite overrun with brambles and ferns.

The cottage itself was in a sorry state, it's windows smashed or boarded-up. The thatched roof was balding and the weather-cock (actually a fox) pointed straight down to the ground.

'I'd like you to re-enact what happened on the day you found Jake.' I requested, as we paused outside the door. 'Did Vicki come in with you?'

'No, she stayed in the car,' recalled Byron. 'It was dark. There was a slit of light in that window up there. I went inside.'

We pushed open the door to find an interior just as sad as the exterior. Wallpaper looped off the walls everywhere, and a damp, mildewy odour overwhelmed the senses. My guide led on through the dingy hall to a staircase. As we ascended it he warned: 'Be careful, man, I put my foot through that step.'

'Oh yes, the wood's rotten,' I confirmed.

The landing onto which we emerged had five doors off it.

'Which room was Jake in, then?' I enquired.

'That one, right at the end.'

'How did you find that out?'

'The light was coming from under the door.'

'I see. And all these other doors were closed as well, like they are now?'

'Yep. I walked down the landing, and I heard a chinking sound, like someone was trying to pick the lock. I shouted;

"Jake? It's Byron!" He shouted back; "Get me out of here!".
The bedroom door was locked, so I had to kick it in.'

I examined the broken lock, which was of a substantial,
old-fashioned design. The bedroom was empty apart from
a grubby mattress, a plastic bowl (Jake's chamber pot, perhaps), and an oil lamp. The single window was boarded-up
with plywood, allowing only a narrow strip of daylight in.

'So this room, effectively, was Jake's prison cell?'

'That's right. He was sitting over there on the floor when
I found him – handcuffed.'

'How did he look?'

'Thin as a bean-pole.'

'I imagine he was rather relieved to see you.'

'Yes, but he'd lost his voice – wouldn't open his mouth
for a while. It was the shock. Delayed shock, they call it.'

'Yes, I know all about that,' I said wryly.

'Also, he was sick,' added Byron. 'He ran out to the bathroom and threw up in the toilet.'

'The kidnappers gave him unhealthy food, I
understand?'

'Must have done.'

'Where is the bathroom, by the way?'

Byron showed me to a door at the opposite end of the
landing.

'So, he ran straight in here and vomited?'

'Right. I waited outside – in case he needed help. But he
came out after flushing a few times.'

I made a search of the bathroom. Inside the cistern I
discovered a large, rusty key.

'Perhaps this fits the bedroom lock,' I speculated.

We tried, and it did.

The ground floor yielded nothing more, apart from a
leaflet lying on the kitchen table. It was produced by the

R.S.P.C.A., outlining the laws against animal cruelty, and the punishments one could expect.

Finally, after making a cursory survey of the garden, my work was finished. We returned to the car.

Back in London, I dropped Byron off at his Clapham flat, before going on to Crawford Street. Mo greeted me with a touching show of relief.

'Sherl! Good to see you!' He said, shaking my hand vigorously. 'No more attempts on your life, then?'

'No. How have you fared with your research?'

'Well, I managed to trace the B.M.W. to a Mr. Graham Parvis, of Welwyn Garden City – he's in the phone book. I spoke to his wife. Apparently they sold it two weeks ago.'

'Who was the buyer?'

'Before you get too excited, he called himself Peter Smith – obviously a pseudonym – and paid cash.'

'Description?'

'Medium height, thirtyish, Scottish accent. Wore a hat. He seemed to be in a big hurry to complete the transaction, according to the lady.'

'Sounds like one of the kidnappers alright. What about the animal welfare societies?'

'Had an interesting chat with John Shilling, who's a press officer for CAFF, the Campaign for the Abolition of Factory Farming. He didn't know anything about the Animal Defence Militia, but he said they sound like a gang who abducted a scientist in Edinburgh, three years ago.'

'Oh yes? What was the outcome of that?'

'The gang wanted all the animals to be released from the research labs. Their demand was refused, of course.'

'And the scientist?'

'Found tied up in a barn, freaking out. He'd been given a massive dose of L.S.D. Hasn't worked since, apparently. Do you think it is the same lot?'

'Let's hope it isn't, otherwise Jake's prospects could be unhealthier than we thought.'

'Actually,' remarked Mo, 'this Shilling bloke got quite aerated about the whole issue. He said the extremists were putting the animal rights cause back years. Quote; "They blow up chemists and put glass in sausages. We use democratic persuasion. But we're all tarred with the same brush." End quote.'

Just then the phone rang.

'Sherl? It's Vicki. Listen, I've got to deliver the money today, at 10pm.'

'Today?' I repeated, horrified. 'But I thought the deadline was Sunday! Are you sure?'

'Yes. They gave the message to my housekeeper.'

I let out a curse. 'This alters everything. Where's the drop?'

'Same place as before; the dustbin outside 12 Dock End Lane.'

'Alright, do exactly as they instruct. Have you got the money?'

'It's waiting for me at my bank.'

'Good. After you've delivered it go straight over to Byron's place and wait.'

'Where will you be?'

'Close at hand. I'll ring you on Byron's number, some time after eleven. If there are any problems ring us on the mobile. And try not to get too anxious.'

'I'll try,' she replied, in a small, unconvincing voice.

Mo glanced at me questioningly as I put the phone down.

'This drama moves into it's final act,' I said, 'and rather prematurely.'

Then I produced a pair of handcuffs from a discreet drawer.

'What the hell are those for?' asked my colleague, tugging nervously at his adam's apple, as was his habit under stress.

'Pretty, aren't they?' I said evasively, dangling them in a sunbeam. 'And a common motif throughout this case. What are they for? Well, this evening someone will arrive at Dock End Lane to collect a huge ransom, unaware that *we* are waiting to collect *them!*'

Mo's jaw dropped. 'You mean we're going to …?'

'Indeed we are – and without informing Vicki. It would worry her too much if she knew the plan.'

'What about Jake? Those maniacs will kill him if we stop them getting their money. Have you thought about that, Sherl?'

I regarded him with a benevolent smile. 'I'm responsible for the cerebral work in our partnership. That was the original agreement, was it not?'

'I know, but that doesn't mean –'

'As one partner to another I must call upon your patience and trust, at least until this evening. We have a trap to set!'

CHAPTER THREE

It was not very pleasant to be lying on our stomachs on the filthy floor of an abandoned Brixton squat, peering at a dustbin through a hole in the door. Especially as we had been in that unglamorous situation for over two hours.

Night was descending, and once again it was unconscionably hot, humid and sticky. The yelp of a distant dog, the rumble of a passing car, footsteps from infrequent pedestrians, our own shallow breaths – these were the sounds that marked out our vigil.

My watch displayed the critical time of 9.57 in shining digits, and just as the 7 turned to 8 we heard the first in a series of purposeful, stilettoish clicks.

'Vicki?' whispered Mo, nudging my arm.

I nodded and put my finger to my lips.

Through the peep-hole I discerned a slender form approach, remove the dustbin lid, and place a large, dark, square object inside. Then the same clicking steps receded into the night.

'The bait is set,' I declared.

'Time for a swig,' said Mo, reaching for his thermos flask which contained iced lager. 'Want some?'

'No, thanks. I ought to keep a clear head. We're on full alert from now until the end of the night. And it's your shift, I believe.'

Little did we suspect how soon the meat of the action would occur, however, for hardly had Mo put his eye to the hole than a car pulled up right outside Number 12. The engine ran on for a few seconds, then died.

'What do you see?' I hissed, pulling at Mo's arm.

'Big car. Could be the B.M.W. – I'm not sure. There's no movement yet.'

'Can you see the driver?'

'Not very well. There's a bush in the way! Hang on, now there *is* movement!'

I gathered up my handcuffs and rose to my haunches, my fingers poised on the door handle. We were both breathing fast now, the adrenaline surging through our tensed bodies.

'It's the woman who ran you down! The kidnapper!' rasped Mo. 'Long blonde hair – has to be her! She's looking up the street. Down the street. Hesitating. This is it – she's coming up the path!'

'Ready?'

'As I'll ever be.'

'Remember the drill. And good luck.'

We heard surprisingly heavy footsteps which grew progressively louder until it seemed only the thickness of the door divided us from our prey. I could feel Mo straining at the leash, but he was not to move before my signal.

There was a clatter, indicating that the dustbin lid was being lifted, then another as the cash-filled suit-case was removed. That was the cue.

'Now!' I cried.

In one fluid action our combined weight forced the door open, and we leapt, tigerishly, out into the darkness. There was a hideous screech of surprise, the suit-case was dropped, and then Mo rugby-tackled our quarry, who hit the path with a dull thud, and another frightened yelp.

I moved in, wrenching the arms back and applying the handcuffs in a swift, rehearsed technique. The whole process could not have taken more than five seconds. Our captive was pulled up, frog-marched back into the house, pushed into a chair, and bound by the ankles.

'You'd better bring the money inside, for safety,' I said, recovering my breath. 'I'll stand guard here.'

Mo switched on his torch, then stepped outside. He returned carrying the suit-case in one hand, and waving a piece of paper in the other.

'Take a look at this message, Sherl. I found it stuck to the dustbin lid. She must have put it there just now,' he added, pointing to our prisoner.

'What does it say?'

He held the paper close up to the torch, and read: 'Dear Vicki, thanks for your contribution. We regret to inform you that Jake Humber died in captivity. However, his death was not in vain. Perhaps now the governments of the world will stop and think before they allow further crimes against animals. We will send you the rest of Jake's fur later. The Animal Defence Militia.'

Mo handed me the note slowly. 'Bastards! They never had any intention of releasing Jake. How do we break it to Vicki?'

'I'll try her car-phone,' I said, grabbing the mobile.

The singer answered almost immediately.

'Vicki? It's Sherl. We're at 12 Dock End Lane. Yes, where you've just delivered the money. No, I can't explain now. Can you drive back here straightaway? There's been a development.'

We waited in subdued mood, watching over our prisoner, whose head was constantly bowed – the face lost behind a mass of frizzy blonde locks.

It wasn't long before Vicki's Aston Martin screeched to a halt outside. She ran up the path, flung open the door, and yelled; 'I can't see a bloody thing! Where are you?'

'In here!' called Mo, wheeling his torch around.

The singer groped her way along the hall, and joined us at last in the front room.

'OK, what's happening? Who's this?' she enquired, pointing at the strange, motionless figure in the chair.

'Our case is solved, Miss Vine,' I announced formally. 'The outcome, as far as you are concerned, is a less than happy one.'

'What do you mean, less than happy? Has something happened to Jake? Is he dead? He is, isn't he! It's your fault,

35

you bloody amateur!' She advanced towards me, her features contorted with rage.

'Please, just let me explain.'

I crossed the room, the beam of Mo's torch following me like a spotlight, and stood directly behind the prisoner. 'This person here is single-handedly responsible for all the recent outrages – the kidnaps, the attempt upon my life, everything.'

With that, I grabbed that blonde mane with both hands, and yanked it off in one piece.

'Ow! That hurt!' came the reaction – in a deep, and decidedly male voice.

'My god! It's a man!' exclaimed Mo in utter astonishment. 'A man in drag!'

'Indeed it is,' I confirmed. 'Can you bring your torch right up to his face? That's it. Now, Vicki, let me introduce you to – or rather, let me *reunite* you with – Mr. Jake Humber!'

There was an excruciating, stunned pause.

Then Vicki moved a step nearer, reluctantly, as if afraid of confirming the fact. 'Jake? *Is* it you?'

I took out a handkerchief and wiped some of the gaudy lipstick off the man's mouth. 'He should be more recognisable now.'

'Jake!' she gasped. 'What the hell have you been up to?'

He averted his gaze and remained obstinately silent.

'I would love to be able to describe this as an elaborate practical joke which got out of hand,' I remarked, 'but of course it's a great deal more serious. Your ex-fiancé has twice faked his own abduction, and cheated you out of a small fortune.'

'Well?' said Vicki, shaking him by the shoulders. 'Say something! Aren't you going to deny it?'

Jake glared, but did not respond.

'I'm sure Mr. Humber would have no objection to my answering on his behalf. Especially as playing dumb seems to be quite a habit of his.'

I struck an authoritative pose, cleared my throat, and then began my prepared analysis.

'Rights… the rights of animals, the rights of men. Jake, here, felt he had a right to share in the fruits of your success, Vicki. After all, if it wasn't for his glowing articles in *Turntable* magazine you may never have achieved stardom. Marriage would have given him financial security, of course, but you kept putting it off. It was only a matter of time, he feared, before you found a replacement; someone younger, less dissipated, perhaps?'

'I've always been faithful to him!' objected Vicki indignantly.

'Nevertheless, Jake felt he had to cash in before it was too late. The solution occured to him when he saw that photograph on your last album.

'Anonymously, he fed his cronies in the music press a rumour that those fur stoles were genuine. It caused a media witch-hunt. Then came the first disappearing act. He retired to a deserted cottage in Sussex, starved himself, and sent you a ransom demand from the fictional Animal Defence Militia – along with a photo, and lock of his own hair. Quite understandably you were completely taken in, and delivered the £200,000 as instructed. Jake picked it up, stashed it, then coolly returned to the cottage in time to be 'rescued'.

'That might have been the end of the matter, had it not been for one casual remark. You told Jake that if the kidnappers had demanded *twice as much* you would still have paid up. A very commendable sentiment. But when Jake heard that greed got the better of him, and he decided to test your statement. He staged a second disappearance outside a restaurant, then posted a demand for £500,000.

'He needed to know whether you were in contact with the police. So, wearing this rather dated blonde wig, he followed you around in a B.M.W., bought for cash. When he realized the Baskerville Agency was involved he decided we must be warned off. I was nearly run down in the process.

'The scare tactic failed, but rather than cutting his losses he brought the deadline for payment forward. You see, half a million quid was simply too great a temptation to resist. If it hadn't been for tonight's hastily organised ambush your boyfriend, here, would have waltzed off with a total of £700,000 of your hard-earned cash – probably abroad.'

'What about this note – saying they'd killed Jake,' reminded Mo. 'He wrote it himself?'

'Yes, that was certainly a connoisseur's touch. A master's flourish. It was the perfect way to stop anyone enquiring after him, once he had gone abroad to enjoy the money.'

Jake's sullen silence throughout my explication was enough to convince me that, in all material points, I was correct. Now it was time for the formalities.

'May we call in the police, Miss Vine? There are some very grave charges to be answered here.'

'Yes, call them. Why not?' she replied, with a nonchalance that rang false.

'You are prepared to give evidence against Jake?'

'Don't worry – justice will be done,' she replied, heading for the door. 'Now I'm going home.'

'Will you let Morris drive you?' I suggested.

But Vicki did not hear.

'Better go after her, Mo. She'll be in a state.'

'What about *him*?' asked my colleague, pointing to Jake.

'I'll take care of everything until the police arrive.'

❧ ❧ ❧

The following evening we invited a few friends round to the Crawford Street parlour; an informal party to mark the successful resolution of our first case. It was a jolly enough occasion, though tinged with sadness, perhaps, at the thought of Vicki's plight.

Once the last guest had departed, and we were starting to collect up the glasses, Mo turned to me with a solemn expression.

'It was a great performance yesterday, Sherl. No, I mean it. You've totally justified my faith in you.'

'Thanks for making the whole thing possible,' I returned. 'I couldn't have done it without your support.'

Mo gave a self-deprecating snort. 'It's easy to re-create a Victorian setting like this,' he said, waving a hand around our quaint apartment. 'Much harder to do what you did.'

'Not at all,' I mumbled, disarmed by the sincerity of the accolade. Loth to appear falsely modest I added: 'It's certainly gratifying to find out that one's theoretical grounding can bear practical fruit. There was always the distinct possibility that it might not. Talking of which, you're probably wondering what led me to the solution?'

'It had crossed my mind!' laughed my colleague.

'I've actually taken the trouble to itemize the anomalies which pointed me in the right direction. They're here,' I said, withdrawing a notebook from the desk drawer and tossing it over to him. 'Feel free to glance over them.'

Mo peered squiffily at my entries. 'I can't quite decipher your scrawl, Sherl. What does that say? Drinking in the hock?'

'Chinking in the lock! Perhaps I should have used the lap top.'

'What's the significance, anyway?'

'Think back to the first so-called kidnap. Byron Silk heard a chinking noise as he approached the bedroom where Jake was supposedly imprisoned.'

'Yes, I remember.'

'He said it sounded as if Jake was picking at the lock – trying to escape. This puzzled me greatly at the time. Why would Jake attempt to escape when the kidnappers had already informed him he was about to be released? It made no sense.'

Mo showed that he understood the point.

'Then there was the paper-chase which eventually led Vicki and Byron to the Bird's Nest.'

'Jake must have organised that too, I suppose.'

'Yes, it kept them busy for several hours, driving from one end of the country to the other. Meanwhile, Jake stashed the £200,000 and returned to the cottage, in plenty of time to make it look as if he had been held prisoner there. However, the plan misfired because Vicki never went to Northampton; she got the publican to read the last instruction down the phone, remember. This meant she must have arrived at the cottage *several hours before Jake intended her to arrive!*'

'Yes, I suppose you're right.'

'Jake panicked when he heard Vicki's car arriving so early. He'd already stripped down to his underpants and disposed of the rest of his clothes, but several things had still to be done if the hostage story was going to hold water.'

'He'd have to lock himself in, for a start,' suggested Mo.

'Exactly! And that was the chinking sound Byron heard – the bedroom door being *locked from the inside.*'

'Of course!'

'Jake's other quirky behaviour started to become intelligible to me, also.'

'Such as?'

'Such as suddenly losing his voice directly after he was rescued.'

'That seemed a bit odd to me, too.'

'It was nothing to do with having delayed shock, of course.'

'What, then?'

'Well, let's imagine the sequence of events. Byron enters the cottage, much earlier than Jake was expecting. He climbs the stairs to the bedroom. Jake manages to lock the bedroom door just in time, slips the handcuffs on his own wrists, and shouts "Get me out of here!" to create the impression that he's been held prisoner. But the key mustn't be found in the room with him, or the whole charade falls apart! He can't throw it out of the window – that's boarded-up. Byron is kicking at the door now – there isn't a second to lose. What to do? In desperation, Jake tries to swallow the key. It's too large, and won't go down! When Byron finally bursts into the room Jake still has the key in his mouth.'

'Which explains the mute act, I suppose,' added Mo.

'Yes, he couldn't risk talking until he'd found a way of disposing of the key. In the end he feigns nausea, runs out to the bathroom, and spits the thing into the loo.'

'Which is where you found it.'

'In the cistern, actually. It was too heavy to be flushed away, despite many attempts.'

'What a farcical situation,' chuckled Mo, shaking his head.

'Yes, but the more *outré* an event, the easier it is to recon-struct. That's because the range of possible explanations is greatly narrowed. It's a Holmesian axiom which still holds good.'

'I'll try to remember it, then,' said Mo, smiling.

'Actually, my suspicions about Jake were strengthened by the fact that, having claimed to feel sick, he ran straight to the bathroom, without hesitation.'

'I don't understand. Wouldn't that be natural?'

'All the doors on the landing were shut at the time. How could he possibly have known which room was the bathroom, if, as he later claimed, he had been blindfolded and confined to the bedroom throughout his period of captivity? This was just the kind of trifling inconsistency which led me to the truth.'

'One thing you haven't explained,' said Mo, rubbing his long, narrow jaw thoughtfully. 'Who was the grey-haired man that drove Jake away from the Italian restaurant?'

'Oh, someone hired specially for the occasion, I imagine. He was no doubt told it was part of a practical joke. Anything else you want to ask?'

'No, not at the moment. Now we wait for Jake's trial, I suppose?'

'Let's hope it doesn't turn into a media circus,' I remarked.

Mo's eyes brightened at the prospect, however. 'Could mean valuable publicity for Baskerville's. And for Vicki's new album – it will probably go gold.'

I shrugged. '*What is fame? an empty bubble; Gold? a transient shining trouble.*'

THE WARMINSTER
ASSIGNMENT

CHAPTER ONE

'Flying saucers?' I croaked, sitting up in bed with a jolt. 'Let's use the more accurate term; UFOs,' insisted Mo, pulling back the curtains to let a column of sunlight into the dimness.

Squinting, I gave a dismissive flick of the hand. 'Hardly our field. To misquote the great man, this agency stands flat-footed upon the earth. The world is big enough for us; no little green men need apply!'

My moderate chuckle turned into a spluttering cough and then an explosive sneeze.

'You don't look at all well, Sherl,' said my friend, backing away with his hand shielding his mouth. 'Perhaps we ought to talk about this another time?'

'No, no! You've started, so you'll finish. I want the whole story.'

'OK. We had a call this morning from Irene Hoyle, features editor at *Science Issues*.'

'An authoritative journal, I believe.'

'With an international reputation. Apparently one of their star journalists, Dominic Gill, has gone AWOL.'

'Since when?'

'Two days ago.'

'Only?'

'Yes, but they're already getting worried. He was supposed to let Irene know if he could meet the deadline for next month's edition. It was a crucial call, and he failed to make it, which is very unlike him.'

'I see. What was he working on?'

'An article about the current UFO "flap" in Wiltshire. No prizes for guessing the town.'

'What do you mean?'

'Warminster, of course!'

The significance was, I confess, utterly lost on me.

'You do *know* about Warminster, I presume? It's the most famous place in Ufology; the UFO capital of the world. Did you never hear about the Warminster Thing in the sixties?'

'Sounds like a low-budget horror film,' I remarked.

Mo's earnest enthusiasm overrode my flippancy, however.

'It all started back in '65. The locals reported weird pulses of energy coming down from the sky. People were even knocked to the ground. There was also a flood of UFO sightings. Ever since then Warminster has been the undisputed saucer mecca.'

'You seem to have more than a passing interest in the subject,' I observed.

'Well, yes, I have,' he conceded, shifting his weight self-consciously. 'As a matter of fact I've been into Ufology since I was a teenager.'

'You're a believer, I take it?'

'It's not a question of belief, Sherl. I *know* they exist, and so do most of the world's governments.'

'Ah! The great conspiracy of silence!'

'That's what it amounts to.'

I grabbed a man-size tissue and blew hard. 'Well, this is all very fascinating, but frankly I'd be loath to take on such a case.'

'Too late, I'm afraid. I've already accepted.'

'What!' I yelled, stifling another sneeze. 'You should have called me first, instead of turning up here and presenting me with a *fait accompli*.'

'You were ill,' whined Mo. 'Irene needed a quick decision. She obviously thinks something pretty nasty has happened to Dominic.'

I gave my pillow an aggressive punch and drew up the duvet in high pique. '*You'll* have to handle this on you own.'

Mo looked hurt. 'OK, I will.'

'Does this Hoyle woman want you to go to Warminster?'

'Yes. Soon as possible.'

'You'd better make a start, then, hadn't you?'

Mo shambled towards the door, looking the picture of irresolution. 'You will advise me, though?'

'I'm always at the end of a telephone,' I replied, magnanimously.

'Right. I'll keep you fully informed, then.'

'Do that.'

'Sure you'll be alright here on your own?'

'It's flu, not the plague! Oh, and as you're representing the agency perhaps you should borrow some clothes from my dressing-up chest? I suggest the frock-coat.'

'Not my size,' he mumbled, slinking out of the door before I could pursue the point.

After Mo had gone I became aware of a weight pressing against my legs. It turned out to be a pile of books about UFOs that my colleague had strategically left behind. For no other reason than to stave off boredom I dipped into one of them, before drifting off into a feverish sleep...

❧ ❧ ❧

At around seven in the evening the phone rang. It woke me up with a start.

'Hi! How are you feeling?' asked Mo brightly.

'Same as before. Or worse.'

'You sound much better.'

I answered that with a torrential sneezing fit, and then enquired; 'Where are you calling from?'

'I'm staying at the Falcon Hotel – right in the centre of Warminster.'

'Expensive?'

'Yes. But there's a good reason to be here. They're building a conference hall at the back which will be entirely devoted to Ufology; the first facility of its kind in the country.'

I yawned. 'Wonderful. What about Dominic Gill, the missing journalist – any leads?'

'No, nothing concrete.'

'Don't be surprised if he simply rolls up. Journalists are autonomous creatures, you know. He's probably happened on a more interesting story.'

'No, I think there's something strange going on. If you were here you'd agree with me.'

'Would I?'

'Yes, it's the atmosphere – threatening, in a kind of indefinable way.'

'I suspect you've been reading too much sensational literature, Mo. Like these books you so thoughtfully forgot to take with you.'

'Read them yet?'

'A few chapters, here and there.'

'Convinced?'

'Not particularly.'

'Anyway, the bits about Warminster are marked – in case you get better and decide to come down. I was chatting to one of the locals in the bar just now. This flap is the biggest they've had in twenty years, you know. Last week two police-men saw a huge cigar-shaped object in the sky. They chased it in their patrol car for about twenty miles! And there was a C.E.2. case over at Upton Bray. Someone saw a dwarf-like humanoid.'

'Is any of this relevant to Dominic Gill's disappearance? Beware of letting your zeal for extra-terrestrials cloud your judgement, my friend. A man is missing. That's all we know. Look for the mundane explanations first.'

'OK. Tell me what my strategy should be.'

'I'd find out where Dominic Gill was staying.'

'I know that already, from Irene Hoyle. He's rented a cottage just outside Warminster.'

'Good. Ask the letting agent if you can look round the place – explain the situation. The poor chap may have topped himself for all we know. You've got a decent photo of him I hope?'

'Yes, Irene gave me one before I left London.'

'Excellent. Take it round to the local shops, pubs, and so-on. Ask if anybody's seen him. Now, I'm going to take a couple of paracetamol and get an early night. Call me tomorrow with a progress report.'

I slept very late the next day – until nearly one o'clock. But it seemed to aid my recovery, because I felt marginally less like death than on the previous evening. Venturing unsteadily into my sitting room I discovered an email had been sent within the last hour. It was a bulletin from Morris, reading thus:

Dear Sherl,

I've shown the photograph to about two thousand people so far! No positive feedback – except from a woman called Kate Chormley, who's staying at my hotel. She talked to Dominic Gill on a number of occasions, in the hotel bar. The last time was two days ago; he was drunk and started chatting her up. Then the hotel owner's wife, Maggie Campbell-Farr, arrived on the scene and apparently began flirting with him right under Kate's nose. Hotel gossip has it that Maggie and Dominic spent the next three hours together in the honeymoon suite! I don't know where all this sleaze gets us, though.

You may be pleased to hear that I took your advice, and went round to the letting agency. When I told the manager that Dominic might have committed suicide in the cottage he agreed to go over there with me. I think he was anxious to avoid any bad publicity. When we arrived the door was locked, and there was no sign of life. We got in using the agency's keys, and did a quick search of all the rooms. There was no sign of Dominic. I noticed a few dirty plates and saucepans in the kitchen; it looked as if the washing up had been abandoned half-way through. There was a computer in the living room, which he was probably using to write his article. But I couldn't see any discs, or manuscripts. The estate agent was hovering over me to make sure I didn't steal anything, so I couldn't really make a thorough examination.

Regards,
M.

Several hours later, just as *Countdown* was drawing to an end, the phone rang. It was Mo again, this time sounding breathless and disturbed.

'Thank God you're awake!' he blurted.

'Why? What's happened?'

'They've found a body.'

'Where?'

'In a field near Upton Bray – a mile outside town. It's almost certainly Dominic'

'Who discovered it?'

'The owner of the farm, Mr. Lambert – one of the people I showed the photo to this morning. He called me immediately.'

'And he's made a positive identification?'

'Yes.'

'Has he called the police as well?'

'Yes. I'm on my way over there, before the whole place is sealed off.'

'Quite right. Observe as much as you can, then report back.'

As soon as I was off the phone I downed a couple more paracetamol, dressed hurriedly, then packed a bag. Fit or unfit I felt obliged to join my friend, now that events in Wiltshire had taken a considerably more serious turn.

Just as I was walking out of the front door the phone rang yet again.

'Hello?'

'It's Mo. I'm standing right by the body now.'

'Are you alone?'

'No, Mr. Lambert is here.'

'Alright, describe what you see.'

'It's definitely Gill. He's lying face up in the wheat field. There's a huge black hole where his chest should be – as if he's been burned by a laser or something. Also a long, deep slit in his abdomen – his insides are spilling all over the place. It's pretty gruesome, Sherl, I can tell you. Less blood than you'd expect, though. Next to the body there's an ovalish area where the wheat has been flattened. And scorch-marks everywhere you look.'

'Any other wounds on the body?'

'Not that I can see.'

'Right, look around the whole site for anything anomalous. Make notes. Be thorough. I'm coming down on the next available train.'

'Are you? That's fantastic!' he exclaimed, unable to conceal his relief. 'But what about your flu?'

'Don't worry about me. I'll take a cab from the station and meet you at the Falcon Hotel.'

On the way to Paddington I picked up a map of the Warminster area and during the journey down familiarised myself with the local topography, paying particular attention to the features mentioned in Mo's books.

The town itself is situated on the intersection of several ancient ley-lines. Stonehenge, Glastonbury Tor, and the Avebury Ring are all close by; indeed the whole area is awash with mysticism and religious signification. Druidic sacrifice, King Arthur, Joseph of Arimithea... the connotations are endless. Salisbury Plain, with all it's military activity, sweeps away to the east, and the notorious, top secret research facility of Porton Down is also uncomfortably near.

Having steeped myself in all this pre-publicity my first impression was something of an anti-climax. Warminster seemed a perfectly commonplace little country town – pleasant, but nothing remarkable. It was overshadowed by a number of steep rises, one of which was Cradle Hill, a famed spot for UFO-watching. The late evening sun made the most of the scene, emphasising the shoulder-like contours of the horizon.

A short cab ride brought me to the Falcon, which was very much as I had imagined it – Georgian, ivy-clad, stylish in an understated way. There were glimpses of scaffolding and girders at the back – evidence of the nascent conference hall.

As I entered the foyer Mo hailed me enthusiastically. He had reserved a room close to his own, and after registering I had my suit-case sent up there. Then we headed for the bar.

I bought my friend a fortifying cocktail.

'That should steady the nerves,' I said, patting him on the shoulder. 'You've had rather a ghoulish experience. Ever seen a dead body before?'

'No.'

'Nor have I.'

We found a secluded table.

'You know, I've still got the image in my mind,' said Mo. 'Hope the poor guy didn't suffer too much.'

'Has his magazine been informed?'

'Yes, I called Irene Hoyle at home. She took it badly. Very badly.'

'Oh?'

'Broke down on the phone. I couldn't help feeling their relationship was more than just professional.'

'Was Gill married?'

'Yes, but his wife works out in Australia.'

'You think he was having an affair with Irene?'

'I wouldn't be surprised. From what Kate Chormley says he obviously had some kind of fatal attraction for middle-aged women. Anyway, Irene's asked us to stay on the case, until we find the murderer. Money no object.'

I smiled. 'That's a phrase you don't often hear nowadays!'

'Well, she's got a share in the magazine – she can afford it. Listen, Sherl, are you tired?'

'Quite. Why?'

'I've asked Bob French to meet me here in about an hour. He's a local UFO expert. What he doesn't know about the phenomenon isn't worth knowing. I'd like you to hear what he has to say, but if you don't feel up to it…'

'Let me have a rest in my room first; just half an hour or so.'

In fact I slept rather longer than I'd intended, and came down to find Mo already deep in discussion with an owlish, untidily dressed man of about sixty. The word 'boffin' instantly sprang to my mind.

'Ah, Sherl, this is Bob French,' said Mo, as I joined them at their table.

'Mr. Rennie tells me you're investigating the death of that journalist,' said French, shaking my hand energetically.

'Yes. Do you know the circumstances?'

'Inspector Ince was kind enough to fill me in. He's our local man – very open-minded and thorough. We go back a long way, in fact.'

'Really?'

'Yes, whenever he gets an interesting UFO report he shares it with me.'

'I see. And what do you make of this death?' I asked. 'Do you think aliens are behind it?'

French picked up the scepticism in my inflection and directed a long, unblinking stare at me. 'Anyone who's read my books will appreciate that I'm no fanatic, Mr. Webster. I used to work in aeronautics. In fact I began studying UFOs in order to discredit them.'

'What changed your mind?'

'The crushing weight of evidence. Of course one has constantly to distinguish between the subjective and the objective – to a scientist like me that's second nature. But having sifted painstakingly through hundreds of reports I can't escape the conclusion that *something* is out there.'

'What?'

'An intelligence, certainly. Beyond that it's hard to be sure. I'm wary of being too anthropomorphic. Perhaps what we are dealing with is a force, originating in another dimension. A force which can cross into our space-time and even communicate with us. A moral force.'

'Moral?' I queried.

'There is plenty of evidence for it – stretching right back to Biblical times.'

Determined to keep things on a practical level I said; 'But you still haven't told me what you think happened to Mr. Gill.'

French smoothed down the tufts of grey hair that stuck out from his bald pate at crazy angles. Then he answered, in a measured tone.

'The nature of the wounds is rather significant. Inspector Ince allowed me to see the body before they took it away. That hole in the chest could only have been produced by intense heat. Also the abdominal incision was precisely executed, organs seemed to have been removed, and there was a peculiar absence of blood. In all these respects I am reminded of the animal mutilation cases in South America during the seventies.'

'Of course!' cried Mo, leaning forward across the table, 'I read the reports in *Flying Saucer Review*. Cattle and sheep found drained of blood near UFO landing sites. Columbia and Brazil.'

French looked impressed; Mo blushed modestly.

I said, with growing impatience: 'If Dominic really was killed by aliens then we may as well pack our bags and head straight back to London. Normal methods of detection are redundant.'

'Hang on, it's only a theory, Sherl,' replied Mo assuasively. French agreed. 'We are all groping in the dark in this field of research, Mr. Webster, that's the fascination. Let's wait until the post mortem before jumping to any conclusions about missing organs. You know, in a way I'd prefer there to be a thoroughly *terrestrial* explanation for this murder.'

'Why?' I asked.

'Aliens killing animals is one thing. Once they start butchering human beings we're into a terrifying new scenario, aren't we?'

The conversation ebbed and flowed in the same sci-fi vein for a good hour, during which time I began to feel feverish again. I made my excuses and retired to bed.

Sleep came quickly, but I suffered nightmares that were vivid and grotesque. It was hardly to be wondered at given the fantastic nature of our inquiry.

Next morning I stumbled down to breakfast, unable to shake off those troubling dreams. My flu symptoms had all but disappeared, however, which was some comfort.

Mo was already tucking into his toast and marmalade in the far corner of the stately, airy dining room. I joined him.

'You're just in time,' he whispered, pouring out some tea for me.

'Eh?'

'Over there – the table by the window.'

'Who is she?'

'Kate Chormley; the woman who saw Mrs. Campbell-Farr seducing Dominic on the evening he died.'

I craned my neck to get a better view. Kate Chormley was a smartly dressed lady in her forties. She favoured me with a rather fetching smile.

'I told her all about you,' Mo explained.

'What about me?'

'The Victorian clothes, all of that. She wants to meet you ... '

After breakfast Mo went over to her table and suggested that all three of us take a turn in the garden of the hotel. She agreed immediately.

The first question I asked once we were outside was: 'How well did you know Dominic Gill, Mrs. Chormley?'

'I'd only met him a few times,' she replied, 'in the hotel bar. But it was still an awful shock to hear he'd been murdered.'

'Of course. How did he seem to you on that last evening?'

'He was pretty drunk. Kept saying how wonderful I looked for my age! It was meant as a compliment, I think.'

'I'm sure it was,' I agreed gallantly, casting an appreciative eye over her neat figure.

'I got annoyed with him, though, because he kept sneezing all over me.'

'He had a cold?'

'Yes, a real stinker. There's a lot of it going around.'

'Did he talk to you about his journalism at all?'

'He said he was working on something big, but when I asked what it was he clammed up completely. He was rather secretive in that way.'

'And how did your conversation end?'

'He went off to buy me a drink, and spent the next half hour chatting to the barman.'

'The short guy with red hair?' enquired Mo.

She nodded. 'Yes, the regular. He's called Lonnie, I think.'

I asked; 'What were they talking about?'

'Couldn't tell you. Lonnie went off duty around nine, and just after that Maggie Campbell-Farr breezed into the bar.'

'Ah, yes. Her husband owns this hotel, I understand?'

'That's right. She sat down next to Dominic and started touching him – stroking his leg. I couldn't believe how brazen it was. She had this really low-cut dress on. It was almost indecent.'

'How did Dominic react?'

'He looked amused more than anything else. Five minutes later she grabbed his hand and led him off – like a lamb to the slaughter! That was the last time I saw him.'

'So you didn't actually witness them entering the bridal suite together?'

'No.'

'Or Dominic leaving the hotel?'

'No. Maggie probably sneaked him out the back way.'

'Where was her husband during all this, I wonder?'

'I didn't see the Major at all that evening. But next day he was his normal, genial self. Perhaps they have a special arrangement – an open marriage. Hoteliers are a funny lot.'

'Look at *Fawlty Towers!*' added Mo.

'Exactly. Well, I think I'll go back to the dining room for another cup of tea. Will you join me?'

'Perhaps later,' I replied. 'I'd like to see the rest of the grounds first. How long will you be staying here, by the way?'

'Oh, at least another week. Let me know as soon as you find out what happened to Dominic, won't you?'

Once Mrs. Chormley was out of sight I said to Mo: 'Do you think she may have been better acquainted with Gill than she was letting on?'

'Possibly,' he replied, with a shrug. 'That doesn't necessarily mean she killed him.'

'True. But jealousy is a motive that we can't afford to overlook in this case. After all, we have potentially four women competing for the murdered man's affections: Irene Hoyle, Maggie Campbell-Farr, Mrs. Chormley, and – last but not least – his wife.'

'She's in Australia!'

'Do we actually know that? Even if she is, she may have hired someone to kill him.'

As we wandered round to the main entrance of the hotel a member of staff hurried out to meet us. She addressed Mo breathlessly.

'Mr. Rennie? There's a Mr. Gill to see you. He's waiting at reception. It's rather urgent, apparently.'

'Did you say Gill?' repeated Mo, taken aback.

'Yes.'

'What does he look like?'

The girl seemed unprepared for giving a description. 'Well, he's about your height – or perhaps a bit taller, medium build ... er ... '

'Age?' I enquired.

'Seventies, or early eighties.'

I exchanged a quick glance with Mo. Obviously this was not *the* Mr. Gill.

'If you'd like to follow me,' requested the girl, heading back towards the hotel.

We entered the foyer, and there, leaning against the desk for support, was a frail gentleman in a panama hat. We approached him and introduced ourselves.

'Samuel Gill, Dominic's father,' he declared, shaking our hands. 'Can we talk in private, do you think?'

'Of course,' replied Mo, 'let's try the lounge.'

We led the old man to a secluded corner where there were a number of easy chairs.

'Irene Hoyle tells me she's hired you to investigate the death of my son, is that right?' he asked, in a shaky, though still resonant, voice.

'That's correct,' replied Mo. 'Can I say how deeply sorry I –'

'Whoever did this thing must be brought to book. Do you have any theories about what happened?'

'It's early days, Mr. Gill. We could be dealing with a random attack. On the other hand someone may have had a grudge against Dominic.'

'Journalists tend to ruffle feathers, Mr. Rennie, otherwise they're not doing their job properly.'

'Can you think of anyone he's upset recently?' I asked.

'Not offhand. He did a pretty devastating exposé of a drugs company last year, but I forget the name. You'd have to talk to his magazine about it.'

'What about Dominic's wife – might she be able to help?'

'Harriet? I doubt it. She's too wrapped up in her own career.'

'Which is what?'

'She's an agronomist – been working in Queensland for the last year. Wouldn't you think she'd want to be here at a time like this, instead of swanning around in the Outback?'

'Perhaps the police are still trying to track her down?' suggested Mo tactfully.

The old man seemed unwilling to give his daughter-in-law the benefit of the doubt.

'What was the state of their marriage?' I asked.

'A disaster. I warned Dominic against it – to no avail.'

'What did you have against Harriet?'

'She wasn't right for him, in any respect. She's a hardened atheist for one thing. We're Roman Catholics. When my wife found out about the marriage she just gave in to her illness and died – within a month.'

I tutted my sympathy. 'Tell me, how did Dominic cope with being apart from Harriet for long periods? It couldn't have been easy. Was he ever tempted by another woman? Irene Hoyle, for example?'

Samuel Gill considered this carefully. 'Let's just say I wouldn't be surprised if he found comfort elsewhere, God forgive him. Now, Mr. Webster, I have a favour to ask. I'd like to see the place where they found my son's body. Could that be arranged?'

'Yes, if you wish. Do you mean right now?'

'Would you mind? I have to return to London by five.'

'We'll start straight away, then. Mr. Rennie knows where to go.'

Mo drove us out of town in a southerly direction. It was a glorious July day – hot, but not uncomfortably so. A minor road led us towards the village of Upton Bray, through agreeable rolling farmland. Just as the church spire hove into view on our right we turned left down a dusty track.

'This is the place,' said Mo, pointing ahead to where a section of wheat field had been cordoned off.

Samuel Gill craned his neck to get a better look. 'Please, get as near as you can,' he requested.

We parked within a few yards of the cordon. A uniformed policeman approached the car rather suspiciously, and indicated he wanted to have a word. Mo wound down the window obediently.

'Can I ask what you're doing here, sir?'

'Yes, this is the father of the dead man. He wants to see where the body was found.'

The P.C. was inscrutable. 'Right. If you'd like to wait here a minute.'

He strode dutifully off to consult his superior – a blond, bearded man in plain clothes.

'You can stand right up against the tape, sir,' advised the constable upon his return, 'but not beyond it. We're still carrying out forensic checks.'

Old Mr. Gill got out of the car and walked unsteadily, with the aid of his stick, to a spot on the edge of the field. He removed his panama hat, crossed himself, and stared fixedly at the ring of depressed wheat where his son had been butchered. It was a simple, moving act of mourning, lasting ten minutes or so.

Meanwhile the bearded man wandered over to our car and leant inside.

'My name is Ince, I'm in charge of the case,' he began, in a low, reverential voice, not wishing to disturb Samuel. 'Bob French tells me that you've got an interest in all this?'

'That's right. He told us about you, too,' replied Mo. 'You're an experienced Ufologist, I hear?'

Ince grinned. 'Well, we get a lot of people phoning the station about odd lights in the sky – that sort of thing. Let's just say it goes with the territory.'

'Tell me, Inspector, do *you* think little green men killed Dominic Gill?' I asked, in a challenging tone.

Ince stroked his wispy blond beard contemplatively. 'Are we talking officially or unofficially?'

'Unofficially.'

'I wouldn't rule anything out – even little green men. Officially, we're proceeding on the basis that the murderer is *human*.'

'But what about the scorch marks?' objected Mo. 'And the extra-terrestrial that was seen just up the road from here? Isn't that a bit of a coincidence?'

The detective shrugged. 'To be honest, the whole thing scares the pants off me. Especially as Gill had come to Warminster specifically to write an article about UFOs. We found a rough draft of it in his refuse, by the way.'

'Really? What was the gist?' I asked, with a sudden surge of interest.

'It was a sceptical article, that much I can say.'

'Don't tell me,' predicted Mo wearily, 'UFOs are all weather balloons, or the planet Venus?'

'Something like that, yes.'

'Pity, I thought he might have come up with something more original.'

'What about the post mortem?' I enquired.

'What do you want to know?'

'Well, the cause of death would be a start.'

'The wound to the chest, caused by extreme heat – that's what killed him.'

'Time of death?'

'Between midnight and one in the morning.'

'Were any organs removed?'

'Yes, part of the lower colon was missing.'

'That supports Bob French's theory,' said Mo excitedly. 'The aliens could have removed the tissue for analysis, as in the animal mutilation cases.'

'Can we concentrate on the human suspects for now?' I implored. 'What about Maggie Campbell-Farr, the hoteliers's wife? She was one of the last people to see Dominic alive. Does she have an alibi?'

Ince consulted his notebook. 'She was working on the accounts in the hotel office with her husband Major Campbell-Farr, between 11.15 and 2.30 in the morning. Another member of staff can vouch for that.'

'How fortunate.'

'But there's another twist which you may want to know about. The woman who lives opposite Dominic's cottage saw a young lad trying to break in there, around 9.30 on the evening of the murder. She called the police, but by the time we arrived the boy had disappeared. Whether it has any bearing on the case is another matter, of course.'

Just then Dominic's father, having finished paying his respects, began walking back towards the car.

'I must get out of here!' he called out, waving his stick at us. 'There's evil in this place. Can't you sense it?'

We looked at each other blankly.

'Please, drive me back to town. I'll catch the very next train to London.'

CHAPTER TWO

'Don't you think it's strange that Ince is so open about the investigation?' commented Mo, as we sat in the Tudor Tea Rooms, studying the somewhat restricted menu.

'I can only think that Bob French has asked him to co-operate with us.' I speculated. 'They're very old friends. And French likes you because of your interest in UFOs. But I feel Ince may be allowing himself to be unduly biased towards an alien solution to the problem. That could hamper his efforts.'

'Maybe you're biased the other way,' retorted my colleague.

'For the time being I remain neutral. What are you asking me to believe, anyway? That the extra-terrestrials killed Gill because he was writing a sceptical article about them? Could they read his mind?'

'There is evidence that they use telepathy, yes.'

I threw down my menu in frustration.

After a pause Mo said: 'But if it's human suspects you want, there's no shortage of dodgy characters in the eco warrior's camp – they're protesting about fracking in the area. It's only a few miles away from where Dominic was killed.'

'How do you know this?'

'The farmer who found Dominic's body told me. He has trouble with them himself.'

'What kind of trouble?'

'They do drugs, play loud music – that kind of stuff. And they don't like people trying to move them on.'

'You should have mentioned this before,' I said, getting up from the table. 'It's important that I cover all the conventional hypotheses.'

Mo looked slightly crestfallen. 'Aren't we going to eat?'

'Afterwards,' I insisted.

The eco warriors had settled in an expanse of scrub, just off the main road between Warminster and Trowbridge. The noise from their combined radios and ghetto-blasters was formidable, and could be heard from miles away. Their accommodation consisted of an ecclectic mix of cars, vans, caravans, and even lorries.

Our arrival at the site was greeted with some suspicion, probably because we looked as if we might be emissaries from the council. Having established our independent credentials, however, we were able to make a few discreet enquiries, and discover that Dominic Gill had visited the place two weeks earlier. Strange orange lights had been reported locally, and Gill had been most anxious to speak to anyone who may have spotted them. A man called Doddy was pointed out to us; he had apparently conversed at length with Gill.

We approached Doddy's customised Ford Transit van with some trepidation, because it was being circled at the time by a couple of rather fierce looking Alsatians. Fortunately they turned out to be harmless enough. The man himself, like most of his itinerant brethren, had knotted hair, and wore green trousers tucked into high laced boots.

'Excuse me, I understand you had a chat about strange lights with this person last week?' I began, producing the photo of Dominic.

Doddy looked up momentarily from the barbecue he was preparing. 'Why are you asking?'

'He was found murdered in a field not far from here. We're investigating his death. Don't worry, we're not policemen.'

'What do you want to know, then?'

'Everything you can remember about your conversation. By the way, why did he talk to you, rather than anyone else on the site?'

'It was me who saw the orange thing in the sky.'

'The UFO?' asked Mo.

He shrugged. 'Could've been. He wanted me to draw a picture of it, anyway.'

'I see. What else did you talk about?'

'Asked if I was on drugs – which I wasn't. Then we took him to the place where I saw the light – over the other side of that hill.'

Suddenly a tall, thin girl with similarly knotted hair popped her head out of the van. 'What's happening? What are you talking about?' she demanded, looking at us warily.

'That journalist bloke. He's been murdered,' explained Doddy.

'Who did it?' enquired the girl.

'We don't know yet,' I replied. 'He had terrible burns to his chest, and a wound to his abdomen.'

'I *knew* something like that would happen!'

Doddy gave an embarrassed laugh. 'Don't be stupid, Annie.'

'He insulted the spirit of the stone,' continued the girl, with a visionary light in her eye, 'and he got his punishment.'

'What spirit is this?' asked Mo, intrigued.

'There's a Druid's stone up on that hill, there. It's been a holy place for thousands of years. When I showed it to the journalist he sneered – said it was just a block of granite. He actually kicked it. That's when I hit him.'

'You hit him?' I repeated, swapping a glance with Mo.

'Yes, and told him to have more respect. He ran off down the hill.'

'It was nothing,' assured Doddy, who was beginning to regret his partner's candour. 'She just lost it for a moment, that's all. She's weird.'

At that Annie diappeared back into the van in a huff.

'Well, we've kept you from your barbecue long enough,' I said, giving a signal to Mo that I wanted to terminate the interview. 'Thank's for the information.'

'Any time,' replied Doddy affably.

Once we were out of earshot Mo said: 'We should have got her to talk a bit more.'

'I think she told everything there was to tell. In any case, I've had my fill of the supernatural for one day. I couldn't stand to listen to any more of it.'

We returned to the hotel to be accosted by a large woman in a sunshine yellow dress which was hardly befitting to her years.

'Telephone message, Mr. Webster,' she chimed, emerging from the dining room and waving a piece of paper in front of her like a flag. 'Which one of you is Mr. Webster?'

'That's me,' I said.

'Ah yes, of course. Here you are, then. I've written down all the details. By the way, will you be dining with us this evening?'

'As far as I know, yes.'

'Oh, wonderful! It's just that the chef has got something rather special lined up today. Well, I hope to see you later.'

She hurried off upstairs leaving us in little doubt that we had been addressing Maggie Campbell-Farr, of questionable reputation.

'What's the message, Sherl?' asked Mo peering at the note.

'It's from your cosmological friend Bob French,' I replied, 'asking us to go round to his house as soon as possible. He's got new information relating to the Gill case, or so he says.'

French lived in a quiet thoroughfare called Founders Lane, in the more elegant quarter of the town. His house was small, though perfectly proportioned.

My knock was answered almost instantaneously.

'Come in – quickly, please,' he entreated, ushering us inside with a vigorous flap of the hand. Before locking and bolting the door he glanced anxiously up and down the road, evidently fearful of being under surveillance.

'Apologies for the cloak and dagger welcome. But one does have to be careful.'

'Of what?' I asked.

The question went unanswered. Instead we were directed into French's den which was overrun with papers and books, and polluted by thick blue wreaths of tobacco smoke. I coughed and screwed up my eyes, which prompted him to waft the air ineffectually with a magazine.

'A smokey atmosphere has been known to concentrate the mind, at least according to your namesake,' he remarked, cocking an eye at me. 'I would open a window, but absolute secrecy is essential. Please, take a seat.'

He made a final adjustment to the curtains, masking out every ray of daylight. Then he picked up a remote-control and aimed it at a video recorder.

What we proceeded to watch was a film taken at night, evidently by a camcorder. In the centre of the screen was an intensely bright orange light which pulsed in a stroboscopic fashion, and was occasionally obscured by swaying branches. The camera zoomed in to reveal a smooth, metallic, dome-shaped structure directly underneath.

'Now, watch very closely!' ordered French, edging towards the television in his excitement. He was breathing hard, and there was a sheen of perspiration on his slanting brow.

One could make out a small figure emerging from behind the metallic dome. It had a streamlined body, with a disproportionately large head, and circular eyes like lamps. It walked stiffly away from the craft into more open country, and seemed to be carrying an implement – similar to a metal-detector – with which it made a sweeping examination of the terrain. Suddenly it swung round and looked directly at the camera, as if aware of being filmed. It's chilling, unfathomable eyes flickered – then it came towards us with an accelerating stride. At this point the picture went out of focus and began to shake violently, before coming to an abrupt end.

French switched off the video. His expression was triumphant.

'Well, gentlemen? Reactions?'

After a judicious pause Mo pronounced: 'If that's genuine it could be the most important piece of evidence in the history of Ufology.'

The researcher flushed with pride. 'I haven't played it to anyone else, you know.'

'How did you manage to get the pictures?' I enquired.

'Ever since that report of a humanoid in Upton Bray I've been camping out on a hill nearby. For weeks I saw nothing. Then, on the Sunday before last, just after midnight, I spotted the orange light, behind the big copse. I pointed my video camera at it, and the results you've seen for yourself.'

'I notice there's no soundtrack,' I remarked. 'Why is that?'

'It's a mystery to me. Certainly the microphone was working at the time, but when I came to play back the film the sound had been wiped. There have been many instances of UFOs interfering with electronic equipment. This may be another of them.'

'Will you go public?' asked Mo encouragingly.

'Oh, definitely,' assured our host, drawing back the curtains, 'but only when the time is right.'

'What do you make of it, Sherl?'

'Well, I'm no expert,' I replied non-committally. 'But from a layman's point of view it's intriguing, to say the least. Weren't you scared at the time?'

'Of course I was,' replied French. 'When the creature came towards me I ran for my life – it was an instinctual reaction.'

'But how does all this relate to Dominic Gill's death?'

French peered at me owlishly over his glasses. 'Just suppose Gill had been approached by a similar creature. Being an ambitious journalist he would have wanted to stand his ground, in order to get a scoop. It may have led to a direct confrontation between him and the alien, which resulted in those horrific injuries.'

'You may have something there,' said Mo, turning to me for a comment.

Before I could offer one French had headed for the door, and was beckoning us to follow.

'Where are we going?' asked Mo.

The ufologist held a finger to his lips, and led us in silence through the kitchen, out to the back garden. There was a shed at the far end, into which we were shepherded.

'A precautionary measure. My house has almost certainly been bugged,' he explained, closing the shed door firmly behind us.

'Who by?' asked Mo.

'MI5.'

I looked incredulous. 'What gives you that idea?'

'The day after I shot the video I returned to the place where the craft had been, to check for physical traces. While I was examining the earth I sensed that someone was watching me. Later, I was followed all the way home by a man on a motorbike.'

'Are you sure you're not imagining this?' I asked. 'It would be natural to become a little paranoid, having experienced what you've experienced.'

French shook his head ruefully. 'If only it was paranoia. A few days ago a man called Mr. Rogers called me – at least that's the name he used. He told me I had been filming illegally and that all my videos would have to be confiscated by the authorities. There were security implications, he said.'

'You didn't recognize his voice, I suppose?' Mo asked.

'No. All I remember is that he was well spoken.'

French wiped the sweat from his face with his cuff, then lit a pipe with trembling hands. 'You're the first people I've talked to about this. I hope I can trust you?'

'Of course you can,' replied Mo, putting a reassuring hand on his shoulder.

'Let's put the aliens on one side for a moment, and return to first principles,' I suggested, as we wandered back towards the hotel through the town centre. 'To know your murderer you must first know your victim. Who could give us an insight into Dominic Gill's personality?'

Mo pondered for a moment. 'How about that barman, Lonnie Stewart? Everyone seems to confide in him at one time or another. I've watched them do it. Perhaps Dominic opened up to him?'

'Excellent idea, Mo.'

'I should warn you, though, Lonnie's memory tends to let him down sometimes.'

'How do you mean?'

'Well, he told me he'd had "a few words" with Gill on the night he was killed. But Kate Chormley said they were chatting for half an hour at least. That's quite a discrepancy.'

'It certainly is. Why didn't you mention it before?'

Mo looked sheepish. 'I was going to, then there was all that fuss about Bob French's video.'

'Do you get on well with Lonnie?'

'Pretty well.'

'Right, as soon as we get back to the hotel I'd like you to strike up another conversation. Try to establish *exactly* what he talked to Dominic about. While you're doing that I'll seek out Major Campbell-Farr.'

We arrived at the Falcon within a couple of minutes, just as a shower was threatening to spoil the evening. I watched my friend's gangling form disappear towards the bar. Then I went up to the desk and requested to see the owner of the hotel.

After some delay the Major emerged, looking flurried and slightly annoyed at being disturbed. He was dressed in sober tweeds and had an excessively lined face.

I explained that I was investigating the recent murder, whereupon he invited me into the little back office.

'We don't get many murders here, as you can imagine,' he said, in a clipped, turfy accent, motioning me into a functional chair. 'The news has spread like wildfire. Are they any nearer to finding out who killed the chap?'

'No, I'm afraid not. There is a far-fetched theory circulating that aliens were involved.'

The Major raised a bushy eyebrow. 'Is that so?'

'Yes. I believe you're in the process of building a centre for UFO studies?'

'That's right.'

'How's it coming along, by the way?'

'We're ahead of schedule, which is pleasing.'

Behind that well-bred, military facade, however, I saw a definite flicker of anxiety. It had to be exploited quickly.

'The press haven't linked the murder with UFOs – yet,' I said. 'Mind you, being cynical for a moment, any such publicity for Warminster would benefit your conference centre enormously, wouldn't it?'

'That would be cynical,' agreed Campbell-Farr laconically.

'You must have sunk a good deal of your own money into the project, surely?'

'I have a number of backers.'

'Were you aware that Gill was writing a very sceptical article which sought to discredit the whole idea of flying saucers?'

'No, I didn't know.'

'If he'd lived to publish that article it could have affected your business rather adversely.'

The Major stiffened in his chair. 'If this line of reasoning is leading where I think it is –'

'Please,' I said, putting up a conciliatory hand. 'I'm simply pointing out that *on paper* you have a motive for killing him.'

'I also have an alibi, Mr. Webster. I was right here in this office at the time of the murder, working on the accounts with my wife. But I'm sure you knew that already. Well, if there isn't anything else, I do have a hotel to run.'

'Of course,' I said, getting up. 'Oh, just one more thing. Was your wife having an affair with Gill?'

The Major let out an unexpected roar of laughter. 'You're referring to her undignified performance in the bar, I suppose? No, it was just high spirits. She has a problem holding her drink, that's all.'

'Does that always result in her seducing the guests?'

'I doubt she was in a fit state to seduce anyone. No, it was just a bit of fun, I can assure you.'

'Not many husbands would be as tolerant as you, Major Campbell-Farr,' I remarked, shaking his hand.

❧ ❧ ❧

I headed for the bar, and found Mo sitting alone at a table.

'Any luck with Lonnie Stewart?' I asked, glancing at the diminutive carrot-haired barman, who was in the process of serving a guest.

'He still won't admit that he had a proper conversation with Gill,' replied my colleague in a low voice.

'I see.'

'But he's told me something about himself. Used to be a jockey for Major Campbell-Farr, in the days when the Major trained horses in Berkshire.'

'So they go back a long way?'

'Yes.'

'Right. That confirms a little theory I've been developing. You stay here – I want to put it to the test.'

I went up and ordered a glass of dry white wine. 'Have one yourself, Lonnie,' I added, handing over the extra money.

Stewart's tiny, chimp-like face contorted into a lopsided grin. 'That's very kind of you, sir,' he piped.

'I understand you were a jockey in a former life?'

'Correct.'

'I'm a bit of a racegoer myself. Did you ride any big winners?'

'Not really big. Ever heard of Pearl Diver?'

'Should I have done?'

'He was probably the best animal I rode.'

'Why did you give it up?'

'Back injury – put me right out of the game. The Major offered me this job when he bought the hotel.'

'So you owe him a lot?'

'You could say that.'

I took out a Baskerville card and handed it over. 'I'll be totally honest with you, Lonnie. We're looking into the death of the journalist, Dominic Gill. Someone broke into his cottage on the night he died, and there's a theory floating around that it was you.'

Lonnie's jaw dropped. 'Me? Why should I do that?'

'I don't know. You see, the witness described the intruder as a "young lad".'

'Well, then.'

'But that description was only based on height. You're no more than five foot four, I should think.'

'So?'

'I understand you went off duty at nine that evening. Why?'

'I wasn't feeling too good. Pat said she'd take over my shift.'

'Where did you go after you left the hotel?'

'Home.'

'What time did you arrive?'

'Don't know. About ten, I think.'

'Don't you live in Warminster?'

'Yes, York Road.'

'Does it take an hour to drive home?'

'Look, this is out of order! Why are you accusing me?'

'I told you – it's a theory that the police are nursing. I thought it was only fair to warn you. I've got a soft spot for jockeys, otherwise I wouldn't bother.'

Stewart looked suddenly grateful. 'OK. Thanks for the tip.'

I drained my glass then stared at him gravely. 'The trouble is, they're bound to link the burglary with the murder. Once that happens it could start to get *extremely* sticky for you. Well, if there's anything you want to get off your chest just knock on my door – room thirty two. Or phone me on the mobile number. I'd hate to see you go down for a murder you didn't commit.'

With that I sauntered out of the bar.

Mo caught up with me in the lobby. 'What on earth did you say to the guy? He looked as if he'd been run over by a bus!'

'I suggested that he was the person who broke into Gill's cottage. He denied it, but not very convincingly.'

'You think it was him?'

'Yes, I do.'

'What was he after?'

'My guess is the Major sent him there to find out what kind of article Gill was writing.'

'Could he have done the murder as well, then?'

'He could have done, but I don't think he did.'

Later, as I was dressing for dinner, the mobile buzzed.

It was Lonnie.

'I've been thinking about what you said,' he began, almost in a whisper. 'I want to talk. Not here, though. Meet me in Upton Bray at eleven tonight.'

'Where, exactly?'

'At the top of the hill – Flint Rise, it's called. Don't worry, I'll find you.'

CHAPTER THREE

We arrived at Upton Bray early, and parked the car in a lay-by which overlooked the very copse where French's video was shot.

Then we waited for Stewart to show up.

The gibbous moon played hide-and-seek behind racing, mother-of-pearl clouds, occasionally allowing us enough light to discern the broad outlines of the surrounding country.

'I don't see why we couldn't talk to him in the hotel,' complained Mo, plucking a tissue from the glove compartment and dabbing at his nose.

'Don't tell me you're getting a cold now?' I asked solicitously.

'Possibly. I feel a bit rough.'

'You should have said. I wouldn't have dragged you along.'

After a long pause Mo asked airily: 'What happens if we see the alien? I mean, what's our procedure?'

'The procedure is to get the hell out of here,' I replied firmly.

'Right. Just checking…'

The next half hour passed without any sign of Lonnie, and by 11.15 we were beginning to suspect that he would stand us up. Suddenly our eyes were drawn to a source of bright orange light on the other side of the copse, slightly above the horizon. It flashed on and off, just as in Bob French's film.

Mo grabbed a pair of binoculars from the back seat, got out of the car, and peered at it.

'Well?' I asked, joining him.

'Could be a plane, I suppose. I can't see any object underneath. You'd better start the engine, though – in case we have to make a quick getaway.'

I did as he asked. We continued our observation from the safety of the car, the light winking at us almost mockingly.

After a while Mo asked: 'How long do we stay here, Sherl?'

The tension was obviously beginning to get to him, because his voice was full of suppressed emotion, and the hand that wasn't holding the binoculars was massaging his adam's apple.

'Let's give Lonnie another quarter of an hour, say,' I suggested, glancing in the rear-view mirror.

What I saw there instantly turned my blood to ice ...

Illuminated by the red glow of our rear lights was what I could only describe as a *creature*. It was small, had a large circular head, two shining eyes, and bore more than a passing resemblance to the being in the video. More worrying still, it was striding up the road straight towards us.

Without saying anything to Mo I slammed into first gear and tried to accelerate away, but in my haste I lifted the clutch too quickly and stalled.

'What are you doing?' asked Mo.

'Nothing!' I barked, not wishing to alarm my friend. But it was pretty obvious that something was amiss.

'Where are we going, Sherl?'

I glanced in the mirror again. The thing was almost upon us – ten yards away at the most. I locked my door instinctively, and shouted at Mo to do the same.

'Why? What's going on?'

'Just do it! There's an *alien* right behind us.'

That word would have sounded preposterous, but for the sickening cold reality of the situation.

Before I even had a chance to restart the engine there was a heart-stopping tap on my window.

Almost incapacitated with fear I turned, and looked straight into those lamp-like eyes, temporarily blinded by their brightness.

The next thing I saw, once my vision had recovered, was the lop-sided grin of Lonnie Stewart.

'It's only me!' he called, giving a thumbs up. 'Not a Martian, as you thought!' With that he collapsed onto the bonnet of the car in a helpless fit of laughter.

I was hardly in the mood to see the funny side. Nor, indeed, was Mo, who was slumped in his seat, having almost fainted away with terror! I'm not ashamed to say that I completely lost my temper, jumped out of the car, and punched Stewart squarely on the jaw. He fell backwards onto the ground, more out of surprise than from the force of the blow, whereupon I grabbed him by the shoulders and shook him violently, like a rag-doll, until I had no more energy.

Then I got back into the car and prepared to drive off.

'Hang on!' squawked the indefatigable Stewart, who had already struggled to his feet. 'Don't you want to know how I did it?'

He did a little twirl in the headlights, so that we could see that he had a wet suit on.

'And this is what I used for the head,' he added, picking up a diving helmet. 'I stuck these torches on to make the eyes. Pretty clever, eh?'

'Who put you up to it?' I demanded.

'The Major. But he doesn't know I'm here. He'd kill me if he knew I was talking to you.'

'Why are you talking to us?'

' 'Cos the whole thing's got out of hand. It started off as a joke, but now it's got serious.'

Mo obviously found it extremely hard to accept that he'd been duped by such a childish prank. He pointed to the orange light which was still pulsing away on the horizon, and asked Lonnie: 'How do you explain that, then?'

'Ah, that's my flying saucer!' replied the ex-jockey proudly. 'If you give me a lift I'll show you.'

'Alright,' I agreed, with the greatest reluctance, 'get in.'

He directed us down the hill and along a winding farm track which ended in a clearing in the big copse. There, in all it's glory, stood the UFO – a Volkswagon Beetle which had been covered with a kind of tent made from sheets and aluminium foil.

'That's a disco light on top,' explained Stewart. 'I've hooked it up to the car battery.'

We got out to make a closer examination.

'How long have you been doing this hoax?' I asked in a censorious tone.

'About a month. Only on Friday nights; those were the Major's orders.'

'And the purpose was to generate maximum publicity for his conference centre, I suppose?'

Stewart nodded. 'Correct.'

'How much did he pay you?'

'Enough.'

Mo prodded at the aluminium foil. 'I don't understand,' he said, 'why go to all this trouble when there are plenty of genuine reports coming in all the time?'

Stewart shook his head. 'The real sightings started to dry up in the spring. That's why the Major got worried, and asked me to help. It was all going great until Dominic Gill turned up.'

I gave him an inquisitorial stare. 'It was you who broke into Dominic's cottage that night, wasn't it?'

He put his hands up in mock surrender. 'OK, I confess.'

'What were you looking for?'

'That article – I wanted to see what he was writing. I thought he'd found out about my hoax.'

'What made you think that?'

'It was just the way he looked at me in the bar that night – sort of suspiciously. And he kept going on about being onto something big. I got paranoid and told the Major.'

'Who suggested the break in?'

'Correct. He got his wife, Maggie, to keep Gill busy for a few hours. Meanwhile I slipped away and did the business at the cottage.'

'But you didn't find anything?'

'Not a sausage.'

'How long did you look?'

'I was out of there by about ten.'

'You didn't wait for Gill to return, and then kill him, I suppose?'

Stewart let out a mirthless laugh. 'I may do some odd things for the Major – but not murder.'

'Well, someone must have killed him. What's your theory?'

'I haven't got the foggiest idea, really.'

'In that case, we'll leave you to play with your spaceship,' I said, heading back to the car.

'If I tell the whole story to the police,' said Stewart running after me, 'do you think they'll believe me?' Suddenly he had the look of a frightened little boy.

'Three to one against,' I replied coldly.

Early the next morning, while I was still shaving, there was a knock on my door. I opened up, expecting to see Mo or a member of the hotel staff. Instead a slim, tanned woman with short, slightly straggly blonde hair stood before me.

'Hi, I'm Harriet, Dominic's wife,' she declared, thrusting out a hand confidently.

'Oh! Please, come in. Have a seat, I'll be with you in a minute.'

'Sorry about the ungodly hour,' she said, sinking into an armchair, 'I'm still trying to adjust to UK time.'

'That's perfectly alright.'

I hurriedly completed my toilet, then rang reception to order tea. 'Are you hungry by any chance?'

'No, thanks,' she replied firmly, 'I don't have breakfast. Got out of the habit while I was in Oz.'

'When did you arrive back?'

'Yesterday morning. Dominic's Dad told me you were investigating the case.'

'You know the basic facts, then – about your husband's death?'

'Yes, although it hasn't really sunk in yet. I only spoke to Dom a few days ago – it was the day before he died, in fact.'

'Really? Can you remember what you talked about? I know this must be upsetting for you.'

'No, I don't mind. He called me in the middle of the night, which was unusual. Said he'd just got hold of something big – to do with this UFO investigation.'

'Nothing more specific?'

Harriet thought for a moment. 'He said it would "rock the establishment" – I think that's the phrase he used.'

'Rock the establishment,' I echoed musingly. 'That could be significant. Anything else?'

'Just private chit-chat. We had to conduct our marriage over the phone, remember.'

'Yes, I understand. It must have been difficult, being thousands of miles apart.'

Harriet smiled ruefully. 'Dom used to send videos of himself by air-mail, so that I wouldn't forget what he looked like!'

'You mean camcorder films?'

'That's right. Him doing the washing up, or watching television – domestic stuff. It helped to keep our relationship going.'

Just then room-service arrived with our tea.

While I was pouring it out I remarked: 'You haven't asked me who I suspect yet.'

With an expression that was at once sad and steely she replied: 'Dominic's gone – knowing who killed him won't bring him back.'

I changed the subject. 'Would you like me to take you to his cottage? There are a few effects to go through.'

'I did that yesterday.'

'Oh, I see. Did you happen to notice if Dominic's camcorder was lying about?'

'No, it wasn't,' she replied definitely. 'Perhaps it's been stolen? I'd better tell the police.'

'Yes, you'd better. When are you seeing them?'

'Straight after this.'

Once Harriet had left I trotted down the corridor to Mo's room, and knocked on the door. Judging by how long it took him to answer he had been in a profound slumber.

'We're supposed to be visiting Bob French this morning, remember?' I said. 'He still believes that alien he's filmed is genuine. It's only fair to put him straight.'

'Give me five minutes,' said Mo, sneezing violently.

Even though the flu had evidently started to take hold he was anxious not to miss any of the action. So having grabbed a quick breakfast we both headed over to French's characterful house in Founder's Lane.

The ufologist was in his dressing gown when he received us, clutching a ream of typed papers.

'Ah, it's you. Come in. I've just been writing to a few people about my film, actually,' he explained, showing us straight through into the study. 'I think the time is ripe to let the scientific community judge the thing for themselves.'

'We have some rather distressing news on that score,' I announced, removing my deerstalker and holding it to my breast condolently.

'What do you mean?'

'I think you'd better sit down first.'

He obeyed, slowly and apprehensively. 'Alright, I'm listening.'

Mo took up his cue; 'There's no easy way to say this, Bob. That alien in your film was in fact a hoaxer – dressed up in a wet suit and diving helmet. I'm so sorry.'

'Rubbish!' exclaimed French indignantly. 'Who told you this?'

'The man himself – Lonnie Stewart, barman at the Falcon.'

'He's lying.'

'No, I'm afraid not. He showed us his costume last night. It looked exactly the same as in the film.'

French shot out of his chair and paced the room, flapping the bundle of papers up and down in his distress. He looked like an owl caught in a cage. 'No, I still don't believe it.'

'We predicted your disbelief,' I replied gently, 'which is why we've taken the liberty of inviting Lonnie round to demonstrate. He should be here any minute.'

There was a protracted, awkward silence. Then the doorbell rang. French seemed reluctant to answer it, so Mo went instead.

'Nothing will convince me that was a hoax,' muttered French.

'Wait and see,' I advised.

After a few seconds Lonnie lumbered into the study, resplendent in his full Martian outfit, torch-eyes shining brightly. He paraded in front of us, reproducing that stiff-legged gait to perfection.

French looked on with increasing dejection, his dreams of celebrity ebbing away with every passing second.

'Alright, that's it. I've seen enough,' he declared, sinking onto the sofa and burying his head in his hands. 'Obviously I've made a complete fool of myself.'

'If it's any comfort,' remarked Mo sympathetically, 'he fooled us too. At least you haven't told the media yet. That would have been a disaster.'

Unconsoled, French pointed an angry finger at Stewart, who had removed his headgear, and was sweating profusely. 'Your puerile antics nearly cost me my reputation! You could have put ufology back ten years!'

'I'm sure he knows that,' I interjected. 'Now, before we descend into useless recrimination, there's something I'd like to clear up. You say you shot the video on a Sunday, is that right?'

French nodded.

'There's absolutely no chance you could have made a mistake?'

'Of course not. Why?'

'Well, the curious thing is that Lonnie, here, swears he only staged his hoaxes on consecutive Fridays. Isn't that right, Lonnie?'

'Correct.'

'Never on a Sunday?'

'No, never.'

'Which leaves us, does it not, with a major problem on our hands. Has anyone got a solution?'

No-one had, so I launched into my own.

'Let's imagine for a moment that it was *Dominic* who shot that alien video – not you, Mr. French.'

'Why should we imagine that?' he demanded irritably.

'Because it would explain all the known facts rather neatly. As a scientist you should approve. For example, we know Dominic had a camcorder. My guess is that when he heard about the sightings in Upton Bray he decided to go along, out of journalistic curiosity. It was a Friday night, so Lonnie was performing one of his remarkably convincing hoaxes. Dominic managed to catch the whole thing on film, and came away thinking he had a once-in-a-lifetime scoop! The next step would have been to seek authentication from an expert. Who better to ask than you, Mr. French?'

'I never met Dominic Gill,' averred the ufologist calmly.

Ignoring this, I continued my statement: 'When you saw Dominic's video you were amazed, excited, but above all *envious*. Here was an opportunistic journalist who had come to Warminster with the express intention of discrediting UFOs, and yet by a fluke he had obtained a piece of footage which seemed to prove the existence of alien life once and for all! Where was the justice in that? If anyone deserved to get the big prize it was you – the man who had sacrificed a high-powered job in aeronautics, and suffered the derision of a sceptical world, in order to devote his life to ufology. Eaten up with jealousy you determined to steal the film and claim it as your own ...

'The following night you lured Dominic out to the wheat field, probably by telling him you'd seen another strange light there. He brought his camcorder along just in case, along with the original alien film on an SD card. Then you murdered him in cold blood – probably by stabbing him in the heart.'

'But the chest was burnt away, Sherl,' objected Mo.

'That was done afterwards – in order to give the impression that Dominic had been zapped by a laser. I imagine something like a blow-torch would have answered the purpose. The removal of part of the colon, and the scorch marks on the ground, both added weight to the idea of an extra-terrestrial murderer.'

Turning back to French I continued. 'Having pocketed the precious SD card you then disposed of the camcorder. A few days later, once the dust had settled a little, you invited Morris and myself to a private viewing of the film. But first the sound had to be wiped.'

'Why?' asked Mo.

'Remember, Dominic had a stinking cold in the last days before he died. He was coughing and sneezing more or less continuously. Those sounds would have been picked up by the microphone – betraying the cameraman's true identity. Therefore they had to be removed.'

French had been listening impassively, almost resignedly, to my statement. Now he stood up, smoothed down his wayward tufts of hair, and announced: 'I'm not even going to dignify your absurd accusation with a denial. We have nothing further to discuss, gentlemen.'

With that he directed us to leave with a peremptory wave of the forearm, rather like a traffic policeman. Lonnie Stewart and Mo trooped outside in silence, but I paused at the threshold in order to deliver my Parthian shot.

'I suppose it was too much to hope that you'd roll over and confess. After all, the only person who can confirm my theory is dead. But be warned; once the police have you in their sights it can only be a matter of time. One fingerprint, one speck of blood – that's all it will take to link you to Dominic.'

'I'm quite prepared to trust in the common sense of a British jury,' returned French complacently. '*If* it ever comes to that.'

'Oh, believe me it will. And remember, you killed him for nothing – for a hoax. That's the supreme irony.'

⚜ ⚜ ⚜

Mo was very quiet on the journey back to London. I suspected it was because he was ill, but he denied the suggestion.

'To be honest, Sherl, I'm worried about the case,' he said, gazing unhappily at the motorway scenery. 'How sure are you – that it was Gill who took that video?'

'The more I review the facts the surer I am. Why else would he suddenly discard the sceptical article he was working on, and so near the magazine's deadline? Obviously something very dramatic happened to alter his opininon of UFOs. He even phoned Harriet in the middle of the night, saying he was going to "rock the establishment". No, there's no doubt in my mind that he took the film, and believed it showed a genuine alien.'

Mo stayed silent.

'Look, I realize you admire Bob French's work, and you don't want him to be the murderer. That's understandable. But the facts have to be faced. Actually, looking back, he rang false from the very beginning.'

'In what way?'

'That business about being followed by an MI5 agent, for example. He wanted to portray himself as the hunted one, the victim. But it was all pretty far-fetched and over-played. You know, if he hadn't made that one glaring mistake – saying he'd taken the film on a Sunday – I may have overlooked all the smaller clues, and we might still be blaming an alien for Dominic's death. It was a frame-up on an intergalactic scale, and almost certainly unique in the annals of crime.'

It pains me to record the postscript to this affair, which is less than satisfying.

The police, at my urging, did agree to undertake a series of forensic checks on Bob French's property. They found a human hair lodged in the carpet of his study, the DNA of which matched that of the deceased man.

Unfortunately, the defence counsel was able to point out that Mo had visited the scene of the crime, and could have inadvertently carried that hair into French's house. It was only a remote, theoretical possibility, but it undermined the only substantive proof in the case.

French's faith in the judicial system turned out to be well-founded – he was acquitted.

Major Campbell-Farr never completed his conference centre, by the way. His backers pulled out when the hoaxing activity came to light. He was forced to sell the Falcon Hotel, and now runs a small bed-and-breakfast establishment in Hove.

THE PERSISTENT ADMIRER

CHAPTER ONE

It was just after 6 p.m.

Alice, owner of the Visage beauty salon, emerged from the basement staff-room yawning, and turning off lights as she came.

'I've cashed up,' said Lucy, her petite, doe-eyed employee.

Alice acknowledged this with a tired nod and locked the till.

Stepping out into the narrow, ancient street they were met by a withering blast of raw November air.

Alice shivered, turned up her collar, and said: 'I can walk you as far as the market-square.'

'No, thanks,' replied Lucy, in a resolute tone, 'I'll be OK.'

'Hubby picking you up?'

'I've got my car today.'

Alice held the girl with a searching stare. 'Well, if you're absolutely *sure* you'll be alright.'

'Sure.'

'I'll see you Monday, then.'

Lucy smiled weakly, echoed: 'See you Monday', then trotted off towards the park, leaving Alice to gaze anxiously after her.

'Just keep walking. Don't look round.'

Lucy repeated this inspiriting mantra under her breath, in time with her quick dainty steps, and before long she had crossed the park, woven her way between the empty market stalls, and entered the passage which cut through to the multi-storey.

Half way along she became aware of that same uncomfortable sensation – subliminal, nagging, a slight warmth spreading from the nape of her neck down her spine and back again. She breathed in sharply, then swung round.

There was nobody there; only ambiguous, eerie shadows cast by the street-lamps. After a few seconds her heart rate returned to something like normal. She continued up the passage, which was flanked by time-worn college walls, trying not to run, but running despite herself.

Just outside the carpark entrance she collided head-on with an elderly man in a trilby hat, who almost fell backwards with the impact.

'Sorry!' she exclaimed, placing a solicitous hand on his arm. 'Are you alright?'

'Yes, yes, no harm done,' muttered the unfortunate gentleman, wishing to appear less shaken than he actually was.

Lucy made quite sure he had regained his composure before turning away and ascending the stairs. She ignored the lifts. Lifts made her jumpy.

Coming out on Level D she was struck by the funny side of the incident and let out an involuntary, whinnying giggle, which reverberated around the whole building. She put her hand to her mouth, like a naughty schoolgirl. Over in the corner stood her friendly little Fiat, its nose peeping out from behind a concrete pillar. Before she could reach it, however, she became aware of a faint hiss, almost as if someone was letting air out of a tyre.

Then silence.

She walked on a few, deliberate paces. It came again, more like a whisper this time, but from no direction in particular.

'Who's there?' she called, in a cracked voice.

She was drilled to the spot, but also tantalisingly close to the safety of the car.

The whisper was now distinct and plaintive: 'Lucy! Talk to me!'

She made a dash forward, reaching frantically into her handbag for the car keys.

'Don't run away!' came the hiss, rising in urgency. 'Why are you doing this to me? I still love you!'

She wheeled round crazily, like a top. 'Who are you! Leave me alone!'

'I can't. You know I can't. Please don't desert me. I need you!'

At last she managed to unlock the car, her fingers almost useless with numbing fear. She jumped into the driver's seat, pushed the key into the ignition, and turned. The engine whined, but refused to fire. She swore and tried again. This time it obliged. Jerking the gear stick into reverse she lurched out of the parking space.

At that instant a young man leapt from behind an adjoining car and bent over her windscreen, his palms pressed hard and bloodless onto the glass. There was something almost spiritual about his pallid face, the eyes were sad and beseeching. For a moment those eyes reminded Lucy of someone...

She shifted into first – the car jolted forward, throwing the man well clear of the bonnet. Then she drove – furiously – for the exit, spiralling down and down, almost scraping the car against the walls, laughing hysterically all the while. It was a laugh of triumph, and relief.

❧ ❧ ❧

'I've come to the conclusion that we must be using the wrong media,' announced Morris, staring broodily into the fire, and occasionally giving the coals an aggressive poke.

I failed to respond, being absorbed at the time by a science documentary.

Mo went on: 'We might have to broaden our net – look at local radio, perhaps, or even the tabloids. Sherl? Did you hear?'

'Mm?'

'What's so fascinating, anyway?'

'A programme I taped, about D.N.A. fingerprinting. Did you know it's a long way from being an infallible technique? Quite alarming, really, considering how many prosecutions hinge on it.'

I switched onto 'PAUSE' and looked across at my colleague. 'You wanted to discuss our advertising policy?'

'Yes, if you can spare the time,' said Mo tartly. 'You're the one who's always complaining about the lack of interesting cases. It's a serious problem, and I'm trying to find a practical solution.'

'You see, Holmes employed what we might today be forgiven for calling lateral thinking,' I theorized loftily, leaning back in my chair.

Mo's eyes started to glaze over.

'Take the *Red Headed League*. It's only purpose was to lure poor Jabez Wilson away from his premises. Once that was understood the case became childishly simple. Now, if we could only get hold of problems like *that*.'

'Tell you what,' said Mo, perking up a little, 'we'll hire an advertising agency – just for a one-off consultation. They'll have a totally different perspective. Actually, I know someone who might be able to help – or at least point us in the right direction. He works at Manders and Bell. Shall I give him a call now?'

Instead of replying I flourished a sheet of superior blue writing-paper in front of Mo's elongated features.

'What's this?'

'You see before you a promising referral.'

'Who's it from?'

'My dear Mama.'

'Your mother?' smirked Mo. 'Aren't we scraping the barrel?'

'You may mock, but the affair certainly seems promising enough.'

'Go on, then. Let's hear about it.'

'Can you possibly contain your curiosity until four o'clock?' I asked, looking at my watch.

'Why, what happens at four o'clock?'

'I've invited Mother for tea. She's always asking to see where I work, and this is as good a time as any. She's getting a train down from Cambridge.'

Mother's teas tend to be elaborate and ceremonial occasions. In order to make her feel quite at home, therefore, I enlisted Mo's help in preparing a sumptuous spread, consisting of egg-and-cress sandwiches, scones, and cakes. We used our best china, of course.

She arrived half an hour late, by taxi. As soon as she saw our parlour she declared: 'Yes, this is exactly how I hoped it would look.'

'Good,' I said, taking her coat and guiding her towards the table.

When she caught sight of the repast she frowned and wagged a reproachful finger at me. 'This is very naughty of you, Christopher! I asked you not to put yourself out on my account.'

All the same, there was a brightness in her eye which indicated that she was secretly pleased.

'You've met Morris, haven't you, Mother?' I asked, as my colleague came in from the kitchen bearing the teapot.

'No, but I think we've spoken on the phone.'

'Actually, I *did* meet you once, Mrs. Webster,' said Mo. 'back in 2000. You collected Christopher from college at the end of the summer term. I doubt you'd remember me, though.'

'Sorry, I'm terrible at faces,' she replied sadly, 'and getting worse all the time.'

'Rubbish!' I exclaimed. 'She's observant, almost to a fault. Aren't you, Mother?'

'Hardly! But let me tell you about this strange business, before I forget the details.'

'Excellent idea – cut out the small talk! You'd better start from scratch, though, because Morris doesn't know anything about it yet.'

'As you know,' she began, settling down to a cheese scone, 'I like to get all my Christmas shopping done in Cambridge – ridiculously early. And when I'm in town I usually treat myself to a manicure at Mrs. Elkbourn's. I've used her for years. Her assistant is a young girl called Lucy. Now, Lucy is normally friendly and efficient. But on this occasion she looked very *distrait,* and she spilt coffee all over me: *most* unlike her. I had a discreet chat with Mrs. Elkbourn (while Lucy was out at lunch). Apparently the poor little thing's had an absolutely *ghastly* time of it recently.'

'You refer, I take it, to this stalker, the Phantom Admirer of Old Cambridge Town?'

'Yes,' said Mother, looking miffed that her thunder had been stolen. 'It's been going on for weeks. This pest lies in wait for Lucy, then jumps out and says *odd things.*'

'You mean obscene, threatening things?' asked Mo.

Mother shook her head ruminatively. 'Not exactly, no. More like professions of undying love and devotion. He appears to be completely besotted by her for some reason. I admit, she is quite pretty, but even so ...'

'Could we be dealing with a mental patient – a schizophrenic, perhaps?' I suggested.

She nodded energetically. 'That's what Alice – Mrs. Elkbourn – thinks. There's Fenbrook Mental Hospital quite near. Not to mention all these poor souls who've suddenly been pushed out "into the community." '

'Surely the police can do something?' suggested Mo.

'No, not until a crime has been committed, or the man threatens violence,' replied Mother. 'She could try for an injunction – but it may not be granted.'

'So, Lucy wants us to stop this man hassling her?'

'Yes, exactly. Do you think you can?'

Mo turned to me for an answer.

'We'll do our level best, Mother. By the way, what's this new development you mentioned on the phone?'

'Ah, yes. Mrs. Elkbourn telephoned me this morning. Apparently the wretched man walked into the salon yesterday – bold as brass! He left this letter with the receptionist, Chloe, then went away again.'

She produced a sheet of grubby, crinkly white paper, and smoothed it out on the table-cloth. The message ran thus;

Owen,

I can't make any big decisions at the moment. Please don't put pressure on me. You know how difficult everything is right now. I'm so confused.

All my love,
Lucy.

'The strange thing is, Lucy insists she never wrote this,' said Mother.

'Which means,' I concluded, 'that the stalker, whose name is apparently Owen, wrote the letter to himself, in order to make out he's been having a relationship with her.'

'The bloke's obviously unhinged,' concluded Mo.

Mother's eyes narrowed. 'There's something even more extraordinary, though.'

'What's that?' I asked.

'The handwriting *is* Lucy's!'

'Are you quite sure?'

'Absolutely. She's confirmed it to me.'

I shrugged. 'Then he must have obtained a sample of her writing and copied it. What we are dealing with here is probably obsession – blind, unreasoning obsession. For the time being it remains benign, but we can't expect that to last much longer.'

'The girl's already a shadow of what she was,' Mother informed us. 'She's lost about a stone, I should say.'

'Really? Then measures need to be taken, sooner rather than later. Will she accept our help, do you think?'

'She's keen to meet you. So is her husband.'

'She's married, is she? Somehow I imagined her to be single. Have you met this husband?'

'No, I haven't.' Mother's tone became gossipy. 'But he's quite a bit older than she is, and rich – so I've heard.'

I drummed my fingers on the table, contemplating a plan of action. 'May I suggest that we all return to Cambridge this evening? Morris can stay in your spare room, can't he?'

'Of course, for as long as he wants.'

'Jolly good. And tomorrow morning we'll be able to interview the protagonists *in situ*, which is usually the best way.'

Dora's is a pleasant little cellar café in the centre of Cambridge. Being both cheap and handy for many of the colleges it is usually well patronised by the student population. Mo and I agreed to meet Lucy there at two-thirty. It was, in fact, her afternoon off.

As soon as I saw the girl I was struck by how pale and strained she appeared. But beneath the surface I sensed a resilience, a determination not to succumb to adversity.

'My name is Christopher Webster,' I announced, welcoming her to our table. 'You know my mother, I believe.'

'That's right,' she replied in a reedy voice, 'she's a client.'

'And this is my colleague, Morris Rennie.'

Lucy smiled at Mo, then surveyed my attire (which included ulster and deerstalker) with a quizzical arch of the eyebrows.

In the end she seemed to decide that I could be trusted.

'We're very sorry to hear about the recent unpleasantness,' I went on. 'Has anything happened in the last couple of days that we should know about?'

'No, nothing.'

'That's good,' I said, kindly.

A waitress came over and we ordered cappuccinos all round.

When they had arrived, Lucy turned to me and asked in a rather naive manner: 'How can you stop this man following me, then?'

'Well, the first step is to identify the stalker. He's likely to live locally, and with an accurate description from you we should be able to track him down soon enough. The second objective may prove harder to achieve: we must persuade him to stop bothering you, either by threat of legal action, or by some other means. Are you quite sure you don't know him from anywhere – school, or work perhaps?'

'No, although...'

'What?' I asked, leaning forward with interest.

'He does *remind* me of someone.'

'Someone in your past?'

She shrugged. 'Perhaps.'

'It would help us greatly if you could remember, Lucy.'

'I'll keep thinking.'

'Please do.'

I produced the letter Mother had given us. 'Can you confirm that this is your handwriting?'

'Yes – it looks like mine.'

'But you didn't write this?'

'Definitely not.'

'Then is there any way Owen – let's call him Owen – could have got hold of a sample of your writing?'

'He might have seen one of our appointment cards at the salon. I sometimes fill them out for the clients.'

'Day, date, time of appointment – that kind of thing?'

She nodded.

'Well, that's a possible explanation,' I said, returning the letter to my pocket. 'Now, tell me about the incidents themselves. What kind of thing does Owen say to you?'

'It's a bit embarrassing,' she replied, colouring, and averting her gaze.

'I know. But it could be important.'

'He says things like; "I still love you," and: "think of all the good times we had." Stuff like that.'

'But you've never been drawn into a dialogue?'

'No, I just run away.'

'It sounds as if he needs help,' suggested Mo. 'Therapy of some kind.'

'I'll give the sod therapy!' boomed a voice from behind us. We swung round to be confronted by a large, solidly-built, sun-tanned man of about forty, bristling with belligerence.

'I'm Trevor Paxton, Lucy's husband. Mind if I sit down?'

'Of course not,' I replied, gesturing him towards a seat. 'Lucy mentioned you might be able to join us today.'

He squashed his bulky frame into the space next to his wife, and immediately took over the conversation.

'Excuse my french, but this bastard needs stopping. We can't piss around with psychology.'

'I understand your feelings, Mr. Paxton,' I replied tolerantly. 'It must be very frustrating for you.'

'There's only one thing I care about,' he declared, bringing his fists down on the table with a crash, 'and that's the welfare of my wife. Nothing else matters.' Calming down just a little he asked: 'Have you got a plan, then, Mister...?'

'Webster. As I was just saying to Lucy, we're going on the assumption that this man is mentally unstable.'

'That's not an assumption, that's a fact,' he returned crassly. 'You ought to be looking in all the nut-houses around here.'

'The mental institutions? Yes, that initiative had already suggested itself. But there are several other possible avenues of enquiry. I imagine this business is putting quite a strain on both of you?'

'We're coping,' said Lucy bravely.

'How long have you been married?' asked Mo conversationally.

'Coming up for two years,' replied Paxton, giving Lucy a proud squeeze around the waist.

She simpered, and snuggled closer to him.

'We're trying to start a family at the moment,' he intimated, lowering his voice. 'So the sooner we get this *character* behind bars the better.'

'I can't promise anything. But we'll do our best to resolve the problem, one way or another.'

'That's all I ask,' said Paxton with a ghastly smile. 'If you need to get in touch, that's my number.'

He presented a business card bearing the name: Mid Anglian Construction Ltd.

'Your own company?' enquired Mo.

'That's right. We're the biggest building contractor in the county.'

'You must be a very busy man, then,' I remarked, hopefully.

'Course I am, but I've got a good team – they keep things rolling along when I'm not around.'

I put the card in my pocket and issued an assurance that we would call, *if* it ever became necessary.

'That guy's going to be a pain in the arse if we let him,' predicted Mo, as we left Dora's and began to meander towards King's Parade.

'He's certainly forthright,' I conceded. 'But his heart's obviously in the right place.'

'I'm more worried about his brain,' said my friend bitterly.

He came to a sudden halt in the road. 'Where exactly are we heading?'

'As you don't know Cambridge very well, I thought I'd give you a lightening tour – ending up at Visage beautician's at six.'

'That's nearly *three hours* away!' he cried, in some distress. 'It's freezing!'

I tutted. 'Surely the Rennies are made of sterner stuff than that? I thought one of your antecedents commanded in the Crimea?'

'Irrelevant!' snapped Mo, buttoning up his coat against the vicious gusts.

'I absolutely insist on King's College and the Backs. After that we can argue.'

In the end I had pity on my friend and restricted the extra-curricular sight-seeing to the Fitzwilliam Museum (where the mediaeval armour enthralled), and the Central Library. The latter provided some useful information about mental health provision in Cambridgeshire.

We arrived at Visage just about on time, and received a cordial welcome from the matronly manageress, Alice Elkbourn. She ushered us past the last client of the day (who was undergoing the rigours of a facial sauna), down into the cramped staff room. After exchanging a few pleasantries about my mother we got down to the essentials.

'Lucy has given us a description of this stalker,' I said, 'but I'd be glad of your impression, Mrs. Elkbourn.'

'I only got a brief glimpse of him,' she replied carefully. 'I'd say he was about five foot seven, slightly built, straight mousy hair – collar-length, with a fringe. He had a rather pointed face, pale complexion, nervy looking.'

'Good. And how was he dressed?'

'Scruffily. Anorak, jeans, and trainers. Oh, and a black scarf with mauve stripes.'

'Did you hear him speak?'

'Yes, he said something about pangs.'

'Pangs?' I echoed, confused.

'That's right. The pangs of love. It didn't mean anything to me.'

'Where were you when he spoke those words?'

'I was attending to a client at the time, across the other side of the salon. I started walking over, to see what he wanted. Then he just ran off – leaving a plastic bag behind him. I immediately came down here to the staff room, and told Lucy. It's lucky she wasn't upstairs, otherwise he might have attacked her!'

'What was his mental state – as far as you could discern?'

'He seemed confused. Almost as if he didn't know what he was doing.'

'Insane?'

'Well, you have to be a bit mad to behave like that, don't you?'

'Quite.'

'If this goes on much longer,' she added gloomily, 'Lucy might crack up completely. Then I'd have to shelve all my plans.'

'What plans are these?'

'I'm opening another salon in Ely next month. Business has been going well and I want to expand. Lucy was going to run the new branch for me.'

'Oh, I see.'

'Now I might have to rely on Chloe instead. Between you and me,' she confided *sotto voce*, 'Chloe's a bit scatter-brained. She's been here longer than Lucy, and I know she wants the job, but – well – it would be a last resort.'

'Lucy is the capable one, then?'

'She's a godsend! Only thing is she tends to get down in the dumps sometimes. It was *really* bad in the spring. She went for weeks without smiling.'

'What do you think caused her depression?'

Alice shrugged. 'I know they've been *trying* to start a family for some time – her and Trevor.' She leant forward to signal that another, juicier indiscretion was on its way. 'I believe it's *his* fault. Low sperm count.'

'That is distressing,' I agreed, exchanging glances with Mo.

'But they've got marvellous techniques these days, haven't they? I kept telling Lucy not to give up hope, but it didn't seem to make any difference. The thing is, you have to be bright and cheerful for this job – the clients expect it. In the end she agreed to see a therapist.'

'Really? Which one, do you know?'

'Dr. Klüver. He's a local man – very reasonable rates, I believe.'

'Does she still see him?'

'Occasionally.'

Chloe Miller was next on our list of interviewees. A raven-haired girl with a surprisingly large mouth, she flounced down the stairs into the staff-room, and, on seeing us, let forth an 'Ow!' which was worthy of Eliza Doolittle.

'These are the private investigators I told you about, Chloe,' explained Alice, rising from her seat. 'They want to ask you some questions about the man who's been following Lucy. I'll be upstairs if you need me again, Mr. Webster.'

Chloe flopped down on the chair Alice had vacated and proceeded to give us her description of the stalker; it matched her employer's in almost every respect.

'Tell us what happened when he came into the salon,' I requested.

'I was on reception. He just walked in and said: "Give this back to Lucy – I don't need it anymore." Then he handed over a letter. I asked him what his name was, and he said; "Never mind what my name is."'

'Is that it?'

Chloe fingered her luxuriant locks and considered. 'Oh, then he said something about being despised – 'despised love', I think.'

'Interesting. Then?'

'Then he ran out.'

'Mrs. Elkbourn mentioned that he left a plastic bag behind.'

She frowned. 'No, I don't remember anything about a plastic bag. There might have been one on the desk, but it probably belonged to a client.'

'I see. And had you ever seen the man before? Please think very carefully.'

'No, that was the first time.' She threw me a worried glance. 'You'd better catch him before he hurts somebody.'

'We're going to do our best,' I replied, with a reassuring smile. 'In the mean time I don't want Lucy walking home on her own. She must have someone with her all the time – especially after dark.'

'I'll do my bit. What are friends for?'

'Thank you. It's merely a precaution, of course.'

Changing tack slightly, I asked; 'Do you socialise much with Lucy?'

'Used to. Then she got into this fitness thing – going to the gym three times a week to work out. I'm not really into that stuff.'

'Which gym does she use?'

'The one in Hills Road, I think.'

'When did this start?'

'Early in the year. Before that we used to go out together quite a lot. Trevor didn't like it. He said I was leading her astray.' She cackled at the thought.

'Was he right?'

'No! We were just having a laugh.'

'Do you like Trevor?' I enquired, ready to be sympathetic if she answered in the negative.

'He's alright. Bossy, though.' Now it was her turn to be indiscreet. 'You know he broke somebody's arm once?'

'No, I didn't know.'

'He had an argument with a bloke in Newmarket, about money. Smashed his arm to pieces with an iron bar.'

'Is this fact or gossip, Chloe?' asked Mo sceptically.

'It's true, I swear! Trevor only got off because the man was too scared to press charges.'

We pretended to be shocked, but really, based on our admittedly short acquaintance with Mr. Paxton, such a story was all too easy to credit.

That evening we returned to Mother's house, which is in a small village a few miles out from the town. She proceeded to fill us with steak and kidney pudding, despite my protestations that we had already eaten.

After supper we retired, happy but bloated, to the drawing room, whereupon the family photo albums were brought out. Poor Mo was regaled with a potted history of the Webster clan, in which he managed to display an uncanny degree of interest.

Over coffee I gave Mother an update on the case. She looked especially thoughtful throughout, and when I had finished made the following suggestion: 'Why don't we ask Lucy to act as a decoy? You see it done on television all the time. She could deliberately take a quiet, deserted route home. But all the time you'd be lurking nearby, so that if the man appears you move in and grab him.'

'It's got to be worth a try, Sherl,' reacted Mo, turning to me expectantly.

'I think we should be able to trace Owen using the information we've already got, without exposing Lucy to risk – however small. But as a reserve plan it has obvious merit.'

'Do you think Lucy would agree, Mrs. Webster?' asked Mo.

'She's a plucky girl,' commented Mother.

'I suppose I could ask her therapist whether he thinks she's up to it,' I mused. 'Yes, I'll go there tomorrow. In the meantime, Mo, you could be visiting Lucy's other haunts. Try the gymnasium – see if they have an Owen on their books.'

CHAPTER TWO

Dr. Klüver's consulting rooms were situated in a quaint tudor building, in the shadow of the towering Catholic Church. A steep climb up narrow stairs brought me to his unpretentious threshold.

I entered a small, cheerfully-wallpapered waiting room, which was amply supplied with the customary unthematic mix of periodicals. The receptionist – a lady of advanced years – sat behind a desk, peering at a computer screen, and tapping gingerly on a keyboard. I introduced myself, presented the Baskerville card, and was invited to sit down – with an assurance that Dr. Klüver would not keep me long.

It was, in fact, to be over half an hour before he emerged, during which time I befriended the lady – a Mrs. Pardoe. Being an avid reader of crime fiction she was uncontainably curious about me, my middle name, and my deerstalker hat.

I enlightened her on each point, and in return she promised to inform me immediately if she heard anything about a disturbed young man called Owen.

During our conversation a framed document on the wall behind Mrs. Pardoe's head came to my attention. It was issued by the School of Psychiatric Medicine in Cape Town and certified that Alexander D. Klüver had qualified at that estimable institution in 1987.

'So sorry for the delay,' said the man himself at last, popping his grizzled head around the door. 'Please come through.'

He spoke softly, with a strange accent – a hybrid, I guessed, of German and South African. I followed him into his consulting room and was gestured into a squashy, shiny black chair.

'Thanks for fitting me in today, doctor,' I began.

'You said it was an urgent matter, to do with a client of mine?'

'That's correct,' I replied, 'Lucy Paxton. She's being pestered by a man – a stranger. He's in his twenties, with a pale complexion, and he suffers under the delusion that Lucy loves him.'

'I see. Has the man offered any violence?'

'Not as yet, but things could deteriorate at any time. I'll come straight to the point, Dr. Klüver. Do you, by any chance, have a client called Owen?'

'Why?'

'We believe that is his name. We also believe he may have come into contact with Lucy – briefly – in the last few years. Perhaps they ran into each other here?'

Klüver removed his bi-focals and stroked his beard uneasily. 'I'm sure you are aware that I am bound by a code of confidentiality.'

I nodded. 'But you must concede this is a special case, perhaps even a tragedy in the making.'

'In any event,' he continued, 'I don't believe I have a patient of that name.'

'Can you be sure?'

'My practice is not *that* large, Mr. Webster,' he said, grinning ruefully. 'I think I would remember. However, we can check easily enough.' He spoke into an intercom. 'Mrs. Pardoe, I'd like a list of clients going back, say, three years. Full names, please. As quick as you can.'

While we waited I provided the therapist with a fuller physical description of the stalker, in case it rang any bells.

It didn't.

In due course Mrs. Pardoe entered, bearing a print-out, which Klüver studied closely.

'I'm sorry – there is no Owen, either as a first or a second name,' he announced.

'Ah well,' I sighed, 'it was a bit of a long shot.'

'But please, get Lucy to make an appointment to see me. She must be under a lot of stress right now.'

'By all means,' I agreed. 'Speaking of stress, we might have to ask her to act as a decoy – to trap the stalker. In your professional opinion would she be up to it?'

Klüver shook his head gravely. 'I certainly cannot advise anything which might aggravate her condition.'

'I see. Well, thank you for the help,' I said, getting up and shaking his soft, rather clammy hand. 'By the way, are you a Freudian, a Rogerian, or a Behaviourist?'

Klüver smiled. 'You have an interest in therapy, Mr. Webster?'

'A lay interest.'

'Well, to answer your question, I tailor my approach to the individual patient. One person might benefit from, let us say, regression, while another could be helped by something more experimental, such as sound or colour therapy.'

'Fascinating. I wonder, what would be an appropriate treatment for the stalker, from what I've told you?'

'Difficult to say without actually meeting him. He could be suffering from a psychotic delusion, but then again he might simply be infatuated with Lucy. Romantic obsession is not an uncommon thing, even in perfectly sane people.'

It took me no more than fifteen minutes to get across to UniFit gymnasium in Hills Road. Mo was waiting for me outside, blowing on his hands to keep warm, and looking glum.

'Nothing?' I asked.

'They've got two Owens on their books.'

'But?'

'One is black, the other is fifty three years old.'

'How far back do their records go?'

'Since they opened – two years ago. The manager didn't really know who Lucy Paxton was, either. He looked confused throughout the whole conversation.'

'I thought she's supposed to be a regular?'

'Not according to him. Her membership ran out nine months ago. Anyway, what did the shrink have to say?'

'Unfortunately for us he doesn't have a patient called Owen. And he advises strongly against the decoy idea.'

'Well, what do you expect?' remarked Mo. 'Doctors have to be over-cautious, to cover themselves.'

We returned to the car and drove west out of the town, in due course coming upon a forbidding mid-Victorian pile, set in substantial grounds. This was Fenbrook, the largest mental hospital in the area.

'Do I have to come in as well?' asked my colleague, as we turned into the drive. 'This kind of place makes me nervous.'

'How unenlightened of you, Mo!' I rebuked. 'Think of it as just another hospital. Seventy per cent of us suffer from a mental illness at some point in our lives, you know.'

Mo looked unreassured, and pulled anxiously at his adam's apple.

'Alright, you stay in the car,' I said, parking outside the main entrance. 'It shouldn't take long to establish whether they've got an Owen.'

Within half an hour I had gathered my information. The most recent patient called Owen discharged himself a year ago, and took his own life three months later. Another trail had run cold.

We returned to Cambridge in a mood of growing dejection.

'I really think we ought to give your mother's decoy idea a chance,' urged Mo, 'whatever that therapist says. It could take months to find this guy.'

'Even if Lucy agrees I doubt whether that cerebrally-challenged husband of hers will,' I replied.

'We'll never know unless we ask. Why don't I give him a ring now?'

I hesitated. 'Alright, but don't try to persuade him on the phone. Arrange a meeting at his house. He might be a little more amenable when he's in his own domain.'

The Paxtons lived in a substantial modern residence on the Madingley Road. We arrived just before eight that evening, and were welcomed by an incongruously tuxedoed Trevor. He pressed a glass of wine into our hands and directed us to the living room, which had a bar at one end.

Lucy appeared in a crushed velvet creation, looking rather awkward. It seemed obvious to me that the display of sartorial elegance was Trevor's idea, probably for our benefit.

'So, what's this fantastic new plan you've come up with?' he asked, scooping up a handful of peanuts with simian enthusiasm.

'To be frank, Mr. Paxton, it's taking longer than we expected to identify the stalker. We need to tempt him into making just one more approach.'

'Are you talking about using Lucy as bait?' he asked, with a perceptiveness which surprised me.

'As a decoy, yes. It could save a great deal of time and effort.'

Trevor fixed me with a fierce stare. 'Let's get one thing straight – I'm not going to put my wife in danger.'

'Understood,' I said, holding up a hand defensively. 'We'd stay close to her at all times. If the stalker appears we move in within seconds.'

Our host slurped down another glass of wine, burped, and swivelled round on his bar-stool. 'Well? What do you think, doll?'

Lucy shrugged. 'It's worth a try, I suppose.'

'As long as you both appreciate there are no guarantees of success,' I added realistically.

Lucy nodded.

'OK, you're on,' announced Trevor, slapping a hand on my shoulder. 'But I want to be involved all the way down the line – or you can forget the whole thing.'

'What role do you envisage for yourself?' I enquired evenly.

Trevor plainly had not thought that far ahead. 'I don't know exactly ... we'll have to work it out.'

'Perhaps,' offered Mo, 'we could set up a kind of relay system? I tail Lucy from the salon to the market, then I hand over to Mr. Webster, and so-on.'

I demurred. 'It would be safer if we all kept together throughout the manoeuvre. Then, if Lucy recognises the stalker she can shout a pre-ordained codeword, and we can move in simultaneously and restrain him.'

'OK, that's settled,' declared Trevor. 'Now we can have some grub.'

The next evening we put the plan into operation. There was, I have to say, a gratifying amount of co-operation on all sides.

Lucy left the salon at 6.00 p.m. precisely, and made a good job of looking nonchalant as she set off towards the city centre. I walked twenty yards ahead, while Trevor and Mo kept a similar distance behind.

Having passed through the market-square we departed from her usual route and twisted through a series of the narrowest, worst-lit lanes. It was a tense procession. To our suspicious eyes every young man we passed seemed a likely candidate for the stalker. Nevertheless, we ended up at our destination – the carpark – without incident.

The following evening we repeated the exercise, only this time Lucy walked at a much slower pace, giving Owen every chance of making an appearance.

Perversely, he stayed away again.

We held a council of war in the pub afterwards. Lucy expressed her frustration at the lack of results. Trevor, on the other hand, exhibited a degree of patience which, once again, was surprising.

'I don't mind if it takes a month, as long as we get him in the end,' he declared grimly.

Driving back to Mother's house later that evening I began to wonder whether our disobliging stalker may have decided to give up his campaign of harassment. The trouble was, of course, we could never know for certain. It was all extremely unsatisfactory. As we left the Cambridge lights behind us and sped away into the inky countryside something began to spark in the back of my mind – a half-recollection of a quotation. It bothered me all the way home.

I was pretty poor company over supper, too. In the end Mother became exasperated by my lack of conversation.

'Tell us what's on your mind, before we all burst!' she insisted.

'Alright, if you must know, I'm thinking about the words Owen used when he visited the beauty salon – *pangs of love.*'

'Well? What about it?' asked Mo.

'It's a quotation from a book, or a poem – I'm sure.'

After a moment's reflection Mother replied coolly: 'You mean *The pangs of disprized love, the law's delay, the insolence of office?*'

'That's it!' I cried, leaping from the sofa. 'What is that?'

'It's part of the most famous speech in the English language,' she replied, with a note of reproach at my ignorance. 'Hamlet's soliloquy.'

'Brilliant, Mother!' I exclaimed, giving her a kiss and rushing over to the bookcase.

I turned up the relevant speech in our Collected Works of Shakespeare. There it was, in black and white.

'How does this relate to the case?' asked Mo, unable to share in my euphoria.

'We can now add an important new element to our picture of the stalker, can we not? Yes, he's obsessed and deluded, but also rather well-read, probably of an academic bent.'

'And?'

'And as we're in Cambridge it would seem reasonable to assume that he's a student, possibly reading English. Mrs. Elkbourn told us he was wearing a striped scarf, remember?. Why not a college scarf?'

'Could be,' said Mo, beginning to warm to the theory. 'Perhaps he's gone off his head because of the pressure of work. Parental expectation – that kind of thing. It's a well-known syndrome.'

'The next step, of course, is to establish which college that scarf belongs to. Do you think Mrs. Elkbourn would help us out?'

'I'll ring her tomorrow, if you like,' offered Mother. 'I'm sure she'd be happy to.'

At one o'clock the following afternoon Mo and I collected Alice from the salon and together we strolled over to a gentleman's outfitters called Bramble and Stokes. This is a long-established emporium specialising in official college accessories such as ties, caps and, most relevantly for us, scarves.

The assistant was kind enough to take us through his stock, enabling Alice to make a pretty positive identification. The scarf that Owen was wearing was from Downing College.

'I distinctly remember that purple stripe,' she exclaimed excitedly. 'It clashed with his bright orange anorak.'

'Wonderful! We seem to be getting somewhere at last,' I said, rubbing my hands together in glee.

We left the shop, thanked the beautician profusely, then made our way along to Downing College. The Porter, an amiable man with an accommodating nature, informed us that they had an Owen Phillimore – a second-year undergraduate reading English, who currently had digs in Newnham. He wrote down the address for us.

'I think we've found our stalker!' I declared, as we came out of the lodge. 'It can't be a coincidence, surely.'

'What are we waiting for, then?' said Mo. 'Let's get over there.'

'Lucy Paxton is the one who can confirm whether this is our man. Unfortunately we'll have to wait until she finishes work. How about a little more sightseeing?'

Mo scowled at me. 'They're forecasting snow this afternoon.'

'In that case we'll go back to Mother's house, grab something to eat, then pick up Lucy at six.'

My heart sank as we returned to the salon that evening. Silhouetted in the window was the unmistakable, hulking figure of Trevor Paxton. He was waving his arms about as if in a heated argument.

'I could have done without his interference,' I said, turning to Mo. 'Especially at this crucial stage.'

'We could come back later, I suppose.'

'No, we can't afford any more delays. Let's just steel ourselves and go in.'

The moment we opened the door Trevor turned on us with a pugnacious expression on his coarse features. 'Ah! Webster! What's all this about finding the stalker? Why wasn't I told immediately?'

'Because there was nothing definite to report,' I explained calmly. 'We simply have a suspect.'

'And you want my wife to go and identify him?'

'That's right.'

'I'll come along too.'

I shrugged. 'If you feel it's necessary. I trust you won't be tempted to use violence?'

'That's what I'm afraid of,' said Lucy, looking at me appealingly.

'Don't worry, doll, I won't cause any trouble,' Trevor assured her. 'That would put me in the wrong instead of him.'

'Indeed it would,' I confirmed. 'Well, if you're both ready, the car's parked just up the road.'

Mo drove us to Newnham, which is a genteel, residential suburb of the town, much favoured by students because of it's tranquility. We found Owen Phillimore's address without much difficulty. His was the very end house of a terrace.

There were no lights on, and the curtains were all drawn. We parked opposite. I got out of the car, wandered across the frost-glazed street, and knocked on the front door. Nothing stirred. I knocked more emphatically. Still nothing.

Returning to the car I announced: 'We may have to come back later. He's not in.'

'Hang on a minute – I saw a curtain move!' shouted Trevor, who was sitting next to Lucy in the back seat.

'Which window?' asked Mo.

'The bedroom – on the right hand side. The bastard's in, alright. He's watching us.'

'What can we do, if he won't open the door?' asked Lucy, practically.

'There may be another door,' suggested Trevor. 'Let me out – I'm going to have a look.'

'I'll go with you,' I said firmly.

Next to the house was an unlit alley, no wider than a few feet. Trevor disappeared into this, and I followed closely behind. About half way along we discovered a back door, which was unlocked. We entered the house and found ourselves in what seemed to be a kitchen, although it was much too dark to be certain. Neither of us could locate the light switch.

'Anybody home?' I called, anxious not to be mistaken for a burglar. 'Mr. Phillimore? Are you in?'

Trevor whispered: 'He's hiding in the bedroom. Follow me.'

Before I had a chance to object he led the way into the hall. By sweeping my hand along the wall I managed to locate a row of switches and throw them.

Suddenly the whole house was illuminated. Trevor nodded his appreciation. Then we started up the stairs, shielding our unaccostomed eyes against the glare. I called Owen's name several more times on the way, but there was no response. The silence was frankly beginning to play on my nerves…

Emerging onto the landing we saw that the bedroom door directly opposite us was ajar. Trevor gave me a questioning look before pushing it open and entering. A broad shaft of dim light penetrated within.

What it illuminated was as awful as it was unexpected. A man's body – fully clothed – was dangling by the neck from a piece of cord, swaying almost imperceptibly.

We gaped at the ghoulish spectacle for a few horrified seconds, then Trevor rushed forward and attempted to disentangle the cord with feverish fingers. But I could tell from the grotesque expression on the face, and the angle of the head, that we were too late to be of any service.

'I'll call the police,' I said quietly. 'There's a phone in the hall.'

Trevor caught my sleeve and was about to make some objection, but stopped short.

'What is it?' I asked.

'Nothing,' he replied. 'I was going to say you should call a doctor first.'

'There's no hurry for that, I'm afraid.'

'No,' he agreed sombrely, 'I suppose you're right.'

I went downstairs and tried the phone. It was dead, so I was obliged to return to the car in order to use the mobile.

Mo and Lucy were naturally shocked at the news – it took them a while for it to fully sink in. Once I had called the police all three of us returned to the house, only to find Trevor blocking the stairs with his substantial frame.

'I don't want my wife to go up there,' he said. 'It'll upset her.'

'We must ascertain whether that really is the stalker,' I insisted. 'Lucy is the only one here who can make a positive identification. I'm sorry, Mr. Paxton, but it is necessary.'

He refused to budge. 'You don't have to do this, love. It's not a pretty sight.'

Lucy climbed the stairs with a determined expression. 'I've got to know – one way or the other.'

With the greatest of reluctance her husband finally stepped aside and let her pass.

She approached the body stealthily, almost as though it might even now spring to life and do her some ill. Having made her identification she came back down the stairs, the blood drained from her cheeks.

'Well?' I asked, as gently as I could. 'Is that him?'

'Yes,' she replied in a tiny voice. 'It's all over.'

Then she collapsed in a half-swoon into Trevor's arms.

CHAPTER THREE

'I wonder what finally pushed that boy over the edge?' mused Mother the following morning, stirring her tea and gazing out at the snow-dusted garden with a melancholic expression. 'Did he finally realize that Lucy would never return his affections? Or was it exam pressure?'

'As he didn't leave a suicide note it's difficult to say,' I replied, 'I'm not a psychiatrist.'

'Have the police informed his parents yet?'

'Yes, they're travelling down from Yorkshire to identify the body,' said Mo.

'How awful for them,' sighed Mother. 'What a terrible waste of a young life.'

'I'm afraid Lucy's reacted rather badly,' I remarked. 'She's taking some time off work to recover from the shock.'

'I think that's very sensible. Mind you, Alice Elkbourn will find it a struggle without her.'

'Which reminds me; I thought I'd give her the news about Owen in person, rather than over the phone. She's been extremely helpful throughout, and it's the least I can do.'

'When are you going?' asked Mo.

'Straight after breakfast. But you don't need to come. It shouldn't take very long.'

An hour later I was in the cramped staff room at Visage, addressing both Alice and Chloe.

'On the positive side, we've managed to track down the stalker. His name was Owen Phillimore – he was a student at Downing College.'

'Was?' queried Alice sharply.

'Yes. I'm sorry to say that he was dead when we found him.'

'Oh God!' gasped Chloe, covering her outsized mouth with both hands. 'What happened to him?'

'He'd committed suicide.'

'Suicide? Are you sure?' she asked, looking slightly relieved. 'It wasn't murder, then?'

'He hanged himself in his room. Why, were you expecting him to be murdered?'

'No,' said Chloe, getting up abruptly. 'I'd better go back to my client now. It's Mrs. Budd – she doesn't like being left alone.'

With that she disappeared upstairs. Alice and I exchanged perplexed glances.

'That was rather an odd reaction,' I said, after a pause.

'Yes. I think the strain must have caught up with her.'

I nodded thoughtfully. 'Now that we're on the subject of Chloe I'd like to sort out one little discrepancy with you – it's been bothering me.'

Alice looked surprised. 'What kind of discrepancy?'

'You told me that Owen left a plastic bag behind him, on that occasion when he came to the salon?'

'That's right, he did. It was one of those supermarket carrier bags.'

'What happened to it in the end?'

'I don't know, to be honest.'

'Because Chloe claimed there was no bag; and she was actually sitting at the reception desk – where you say Owen left it. Odd, isn't it?'

'I don't see why she should lie about something like that.'

'No, nor do I. Perhaps you could ask her to come down again when she has a second. I'd like to have another chat with her – in private.'

'Of course. I'll get her now.'

Chloe returned after a few minutes looking very defensive, even scared. I decided the best way to get the truth out of her was to go on the attack immediately.

'What happened to that carrier bag, Chloe?' I asked sternly. 'You know – the one Owen gave you? I want a straight answer this time.'

She folded her arms and pursed her lips obdurately.

'Look, a man is dead. You could be in serious trouble – very serious trouble – if you conceal anything that is relevant. Surely you understand that? Wouldn't it be better to deal with me, rather than the police?'

Suddenly the girl's unyielding expression crumpled, and she burst into a storm of tears.

I remained impassive.

Having recovered her composure a little she got up from her seat, went over to a locker, and withdrew a plain, white plastic bag.

'There!' she cried, tossing it at me. 'Are you satisfied?'

Inside was a photograph album containing dozens of snaps of Lucy Paxton, in a variety of settings: gambolling in a park, walking through a college court, enjoying a meal in a restaurant. My attention was particularly drawn to a shot of her reposing in a punt, taken by someone standing at the other end. She was wearing a revealing dress and pouting provocatively.

But the real bombshell came when I turned to the very last page of the album. Here was a black and white photo of Lucy strolling along a sea-front, hand-in-hand with a young man who looked disturbingly like Owen Phillimore.

When I saw that I began to feel rather sick. At a stroke the entire case had been turned on its head.

'This is a vital piece of evidence – why on earth did you hold it back?' I demanded, glaring at Chloe.

'It was a shock – finding out Lucy really *was* seeing Owen,' she replied, sniffing and dabbing at her red eyes with a handkerchief. 'I didn't want to get her into any trouble.'

'With Trevor, you mean?'

'Yes. He'll go mad when he sees those. He's incredibly jealous. And violent.'

'So, in order to protect Lucy you hid the photos, and went along with her pretence that she didn't know Owen?'

'Yes.'

'And let everyone go on believing the poor chap was some kind of deluded psychopath?'

'Yes.'

'And now he's committed suicide.'

'What else could I do?' she wailed.

'Does Lucy know about the photos?'

'No, I haven't shown them to her.'

'Perhaps you've been saving them for a rainy day?'

'What do you mean?' asked Chloe, manufacturing an offended expression.

'Well, you could easily have blackmailed her with them – forced her to turn down that manager's job, so that you could have it instead. However, I'm not particularly interested in your motives at the moment.'

I picked up the album and headed for the door.

'Where are you going?'

'To confront Lucy. She's got one hell of a lot of explaining to do.'

I was just setting off in the car for Lucy's house when the mobile buzzed.

'Hello, is that Mr. Webster?'

'Speaking.'

'It's Mrs. Pardoe here – Dr. Klüver's secretary. Do you remember me?'

'Yes, of course. How can I help?'

'Something very odd is going on.'

'Can you be more specific?'

'It's difficult to explain on the telephone. Could you come over to the surgery?'

'I'm very busy at the moment, Mrs. Pardoe,' I said. 'Won't it wait till this afternoon?'

'Not really.'

'Alright,' I agreed with a sigh, 'I'll be there in about ten minutes.'

I did a U-turn and drove over to Klüver's little establishment next to the Catholic Church. As I walked through the reception door Mrs. Pardoe looked up from her desk and let out an exclamation of relief. She seemed most agitated.

'Right, so what's the trouble?' I asked in a soothing voice.

'It's Dr. Klüver. I'm very concerned about him.'

'Tell me the whole story.'

'Well, I arrived a bit earlier than normal this morning,' began the old girl in a quaky voice. 'Dr. Klüver already had somebody in with him – which was strange, because his first patient wasn't due until ten o'clock. It didn't sound at all like a consultation, more like an argument. I'm afraid I listened at the door.'

'And what did you hear?' I asked.

'Dr. Klüver said: "You can't scare me. I don't want any part of this." Then the other man started shouting and swearing at him. There was a lot of bumping and banging about – as if they were fighting each other. I got alarmed and went out into the street to find a policeman.'

'Couldn't you have phoned the police from the office?'

'I wasn't thinking straight.'

'I see. Please go on.'

'Well, I must have been looking for about ten minutes – without luck. Then, just as I was returning to the surgery Dr. Klüver came out of the street door and walked straight past me without saying a word! I called after him, but he wouldn't stop.'

'How did he look?'

'Very peculiar – staring into space. He'd left this note on my desk.'

She showed me a slip of paper bearing the following hurriedly dashed off message:

SICK. GONE HOME. PLEASE CANCEL ALL
APPOINTMENTS.

'I still had your card, so I decided to telephone you. What do you think it means, Mr. Webster?'

I reflected for a while. 'Where does Dr. Klüver live?'

'Trumpington.'

'So he might be home by now?'

'Oh yes.'

'I should give him a call.'

Mrs. Pardoe hesitated. 'But what do I say? I don't like to pry.'

'Simply enquire after his health.'

I handed her the receiver as an encouragement. 'Go on – it's the only way to find out what's happening.'

She nodded, and dialled the number. After an eternity of ringing Klüver answered, and a short conversation ensued. He did most of the talking.

'Well, what's the verdict?' I enquired, after Mrs. Pardoe had hung up.

She frowned. 'He sounded drunk – extremely drunk. He said he didn't know when he was coming back to work – maybe never. I asked why. He said he'd got himself into a terrible mess, but that he would get even.'

'Get even?' I repeated. 'With whom?'

'He didn't say.'

'Well, this certainly is a curious turn of events. You were right to let me know.'

'But what's to be done?'

'I should go home and try to relax. Staying on here will serve no purpose. If you give me Dr. Klüver's address I'll look in on him some time this afternoon.'

I returned to the car and resumed my journey across town to Lucy's house. On the way I called Mo and brought him up to date concerning the incriminating photograph.

'So Lucy did know Owen – she's been lying to us all along?' he reacted hotly.

'That's what it looks like, yes.'

'What are we going to do about it?'

'I'm driving over there now – to see what she has to say for herself.'

'Can I join you?'

'No, I'd like you to research this Dr. Klüver for me. He's been behaving in an eccentric fashion today. Ring up the Institute of Psychiatric Medicine in Cape Town. Find out anything you can about him. I'll ring again in about an hour.'

Lucy came to the door of her house in Madingley Road wearing a dressing gown, and without a trace of make-up on her pale, delicate face.

'Oh, it's you,' she said, hardly able to muster a smile.

'May I come in?'

'Yes, if you want.'

We went through into the living room.

'Would you like a drink?' she offered vaguely, hovering near the bar.

'No thanks. The reason I'm here, Lucy, is this,' I said, handing over the photo album without preamble.

'What is it?' she asked innocently.

'Take a look inside – the last page especially.'

Her large round eyes grew even larger as she surveyed the contents. 'Where did you get this?'

'Owen Phillimore handed it in to the salon. You lied about not knowing him, didn't you? Perhaps the reason was understandable – you were afraid of Trevor's reaction. But the result was the tragic death of a bright young man. You'll have to live with that for the rest of your life.'

'No!' shouted Lucy, throwing the album onto the floor. 'You're wrong! I didn't know him.'

'What's the point in denying it? That photograph is conclusive.'

'It's a fake. They're all fakes. They've got to be.'

'You don't really expect me to believe that?'

'It's the truth!' she cried, pulling at my arm. 'I don't remember being in any of those places. I haven't been in a punt since I was a girl.'

She grabbed the telephone and started dialling feverishly.

'Who are you calling?' I asked.

'My husband. I want to explain everything to him – before you do.'

Eventually she got through to Trevor's office. From the ensuing conversation I gathered he wasn't in, and hadn't been all day. No-one knew where he was.

Just as Lucy came off the phone there was the sound of a key turning in the front door.

'Ah, that must be him!' she exclaimed, rushing out into the hall.

'Hello, princess,' came Trevor's stentorian voice, a few seconds later. 'I bought some flowers; to cheer you up.'

'Where have you been?' asked Lucy. 'You weren't at work.'

At that point Trevor walked into the living room and caught sight of me.

'Oh, Mr. Webster again. Come for your wages? I put a cheque in the post yesterday.'

'He hasn't come for that,' said Lucy, picking up the album from the carpet.

'What then?'

'He brought this. There are some photos of me – but they're fakes. Take a look for yourself.'

Trevor turned the first few pages with an inscrutable expression, but when he saw the most damning shot he flushed and glared at his wife accusingly.

'How can that be a fake?' he demanded.

'Owen must have put my face onto someone else's body,' theorized Lucy desperately. 'I'm sure it can be done.'

Trevor mulled over this far-fetched explanation for some time.

'Yes,' he said at last, snapping the album shut, 'it must be trick photography.'

'Are you serious?' I asked incredulously.

'My wife does not lie,' stated Trevor, slowly and emphatically.

Before I could argue any further he guided Lucy out of the room. 'You'd better get some rest upstairs, love. You know what the doctor said – you mustn't get overtired.' Turning back to me he added: 'I think it's best if you go now.'

'Very well,' I replied with a shrug. 'If that's the way you want it. Could I possibly use your phone before I leave?'

'Help yourself.'

I called Mother's house again and asked Mo to give me the results of his South African research.

'Interesting stuff, Sherl!' declared my colleague. 'Apparently Klüver never completed his course at the Institute. He was booted out!'

'What for?'

'There was a scandal involving a female patient. He abused her while she was hypnotised.'

'Does that mean he's not really a doctor?'

'No more than I am. Also, somebody else from England was making enquiries about him only a few months ago.'

'Who?'

'No name given.'

'I see. Listen, Mo, I'd like you to meet me at Klüver's house – you can borrows Mother's car. He lives in Trumpington. Number eight, Gladstone Close. Start right away.'

I gathered up my coat and the photo album and headed for the door.

Trevor, who had overheard the whole conversation, said: 'Why are you making more work for yourself? Your job is over. The stalker is dead.'

'I know, but there's a loose end that has to be tied up – for my own satisfaction more than anything else. Don't worry, I won't charge for my time.'

'I should bloody well think not,' he muttered, pouring himself a drink.

Klüver's house was suburban and unexceptional. His car was in the garage, which was a hopeful sign. I buzzed at the door. There was no reply, so I went around the back, peering in through all the windows. The lounge curtains were drawn, but there was a gap through which I could just discern someone, presumably Klüver, lying on the sofa. I tapped on the glass, but he did not move. Fortunately the french windows were unlocked, so I effected my entry, as silently as possible.

I need not have used stealth, however, because Klüver was in an intoxicated slumber, surrounded by empty bottles of wine and whisky. I sat in an easy chair and kept a vigil over him, while the last wan rays of the winter sun played against the walls.

It gave me a chance to consider the various pieces of the jigsaw which made up this complex case, and fit them together so as to make an acceptable whole.

By the time Mo arrived, some twenty minutes later, I felt I had made significant headway in that direction. I showed my colleague straight into the living room.

'This is our *soi disant* doctor,' I declared, pointing to the snoring figure.

Mo bent down to examine him. 'Looks as if he's had a skinful.'

'He has. It will be quite a task to revive him. I may need your help.'

'You know, there's one question I've been asking myself all the way here,' said Mo, eyeing me intently.

'What's that?'

'Is there a link between the fact that Klüver's a fake, and the business between Owen and Lucy? Presumably there is, otherwise we wouldn't be here.'

I smiled. 'Very astute of you, Mo. Yes, I believe there is such a link – but I won't be in a position to confirm it until we've spoken to our inebriated friend. So would you be kind enough to get a jug of cold water from the kitchen?'

'To pour over him?'

'The old methods are the best. Oh, and you might make a pot of strong coffee as well.'

In fact it required more than one jugful of icy water, and several hard slaps to the face, to bring Klüver round. He sat up suddenly, rubbing his grizzled head, and groaning slightly. 'Here, drink this,' I ordered, shoving a mug of steaming coffee into his hands. 'My name is Webster; I came to see you about Lucy Paxton – do you remember?'

He nodded, and even that small effort caused him to wince with pain.

'My associate, here, has been trying to establish your *bona fides,* doctor. The Institute in Cape Town were very forthcoming. We know that you're a charlatan, and that you've been up to your old tricks again.'

'What do you mean by that?' he asked, putting on his glasses and squinting at me.

'You've been hypnotising patients and abusing them.'

'How dare you!' he exclaimed.

'It's a different kind of abuse this time,' I went on. 'Not touching up female clients, something much more sinister.'

'What are you talking about?'

'I'm referring to Lucy, of course. You used hypnotic techniques to make her believe that Owen Phillimore was a total stranger, even though they'd been lovers for months. You systematically washed away all her memories of him. I call that abuse.'

'What possible reason could I have for doing such a thing?' objected Klüver, sobering up by the second. 'It doesn't make any sense. Anyway, how do you know she was having a relationship with Owen?'

I produced the photo album and pointed to the relevant pages. The faintest flicker of indecision passed across

Klüver's pasty features. 'This is all news to me – I had no idea.'

'I don't believe you. However, you're right to say that you have no motive for tampering with Lucy's mind.'

'Exactly!' exclaimed Klüver indignantly.

'Which leads me to believe you were acting on behalf of a third party – probably under coercion. After all, a man who goes around pretending to be something he isn't is extremely vulnerable to coercion.'

'Who is this third party you're talking about?'

'Someone you're afraid of; someone who's already murdered one man; someone who wouldn't stick at murdering you if it became necessary.'

Just at that moment there was a thunderous series of knocks on the front door, which caused Klüver to jump nearly out of his skin. The timing was impeccable.

'No doubt that's the individual now,' I remarked. 'Would you like us to hide nearby – in case there's trouble?'

Klüver did not object to the idea; in fact he seemed relieved that he would not have to face the situation alone.

Mo and I took up strategic positions in the kitchen. I made sure the hatch which connected it with the lounge was slightly ajar, so that we could keep an eye on proceedings.

We heard Klüver walk along to the front door, open it, and mumble a greeting.

A few seconds later a familiar, more robust voice rang out in the hallway: 'Have you been on the piss?'

'I've had a few drinks, yes,' replied Klüver in an apologetic tone.

As I peered through the hatch the burly form of Trevor Paxton lumbered into view.

'Has Webster been here?' he demanded.

'He came and went,' replied Klüver airily.

'What did you tell him?'

'Nothing he didn't already know.'

'What do you mean by that?' asked Paxton sharply.

'He's found out that I hypnotised Lucy. And that you blackmailed me into doing it. He even knows that you forced Owen to put his head in that noose.'

'How does he know?'

'I've got absolutely no idea.'

'I think you must have told him yourself,' concluded Paxton, in a quietly menacing manner.

Suddenly his huge hands were around the older man's throat and they both fell back onto the sofa in a deadly embrace.

Feeling this might be a propitious time to intervene I rushed through into the lounge, followed closely by Mo. Paxton looked utterly astonished when he saw us, but his grip on poor Klüver – whose face had by now turned an alarming shade of purple – did not weaken. Mo pulled at one of Paxton's arms, I the other, and eventually we managed to prize him loose. With a growl of anger he lashed out at both of us simultaneously, knocking us aside, before running down the hall and out of the house.

'Shall we go after him?' cried Mo, picking himself up from the floor.

'No! It's more important that we get to Lucy,' I replied.

'Why?'

'He might grab her and try to leave the country. She still has absolute faith in him, remember.'

'Take me to her,' gasped the half-throttled Klüver. 'I'm the only one who can make her see sense.'

I considered the suggestion for a moment. 'Will you admit to her what you've done?'

He nodded emphatically. 'Everything – I'll tell her everything.'

'Very well. Help him into the car, would you, Mo?'

By the time we set off up Trumpington Road the therapist's face had returned to an acceptable hue, but he was still finding it hard to catch his breath.

'Are you sure you're alright?' I asked him humanely. 'We can stop off at the hospital if you want.'

'No, there's no time. Keep going.'

I took the quickest route I knew through the town. While we were waiting at traffic lights I phoned Lucy and advised her to lock herself in, and not to open the door to anyone until we arrived.

'Not even my husband?' she asked in surprise.

'Especially not your husband.'

'Why? What's going on?'

'I can't explain now, but you must do as I say.'

She agreed, albeit grudgingly.

Eventually we turned into the Paxtons' drive, and to my great relief Trevor's car was nowhere to be seen. Lucy was gazing down at us from a bedroom window.

A few seconds later she emerged from the front door looking bewildered. 'What's all this about? Why have you brought Dr. Klüver with you?'

'He has something very important to say,' I explained. 'But as you can see, he's not feeling very well. Could we go inside?'

Lucy led the way into the drawing room and sat Klüver down on the sofa.

'What's the matter with him?' she enquired, inspecting his neck. 'How did he get these marks?'

'You may well ask,' I replied, aiming a glance at Mo.

'Is that what you've come to talk to me about?'

'Not exactly, no.'

'What then? Not those photos again, I hope?'

'Dr. Klüver, here, would like to make a confession.'

Lucy's brow puckered into a confused frown. 'What kind of confession?'

The therapist cleared his throat, and then looked her straight in the eye. 'Originally you came to me complaining of depression, do you remember?'

'Yes. So?'

'That depression wasn't caused by your failure to conceive a child with Trevor – as you now believe.'

'What, then?'

'The truth is, you never really loved him, and you felt trapped in the marriage. This led to you having an affair with Owen Phillimore, which in turn made you feel confused and guilty.'

'Why are you lying?' shouted Lucy, stamping her foot petulantly. 'I never knew Owen Phillimore.'

'Please, hear him out,' I entreated. 'Carry on, doctor.'

Klüver smiled wryly. 'That's the trouble; I'm not really a doctor at all – I never qualified. Trevor found out. He came to me one evening and threatened to expose me unless I did exactly what he asked. He already knew you were seeing Owen, and he wanted me to make you stop – using hypnosis. I was in no position to refuse.

'Because you're such an excellent, suggestible subject it took only a few sessions to turn you into something you weren't – a happy, devoted wife. The next stage was to suppress all your memories of Owen. That took longer – but I succeeded in the end. Unfortunately, the young man refused to be put off. He couldn't understand why you had suddenly spurned him. He began hounding you in the street.'

'Which is where we came in,' I said, taking up the story. 'If we'd talked to Owen he may well have been able to persuade us that your behaviour was unnatural – that something very odd was going on. Trevor knew that, and couldn't risk it. That's why he murdered him.'

'Trevor didn't murder anyone,' exclaimed Lucy. 'It was suicide – I saw it with my own eyes.'

'That's how it was made to look, certainly. But there was no note. You'd expect a clever, literary chap like Owen to put a few words together for the occasion, wouldn't you?'

'Lot's of people kill themselves without leaving notes,' protested Lucy.

'All the same, it was indicative. And there was something else that made me suspicious. Just after we discovered the body I was about to go downstairs to phone the police. Trevor instinctively reached out to stop me, and then checked himself. You see, he already *knew* the telephone in Owen's hall wasn't working – because he'd been in the flat before. Yet why should he have been there, if it wasn't to murder him?'

'I know my husband couldn't kill anyone,' said Lucy with unshakable conviction. 'You haven't got any proof, anyway.'

'The police will be able to link him to the murder forensically,' I assured her. 'You can't force someone to hang themselves without leaving some trace. The trouble is he returned to the scene with me, probably wearing the same clothes. That was clever, because now anything they do find can be attributed to the second, innocent visit, rather than the first.'

'I have proof,' said Klüver calmly.

We all turned to him in surprise.

'Well, I needed to have some way of clearing my name, in case all this came out. So I secretly taped our conversations.' He addressed Lucy solemnly. 'Your husband explicitly admits to the killing on one of the tapes; it's safely lodged with my solicitor, if you want to hear it.'

Poor Lucy seemed momentarily rocked by this new revelation, but she quickly recovered her composure. 'Tapes can be faked, just like photos.'

I smiled, and placed an avuncular hand on her arm. 'Look, Lucy, the reason you won't hear a word against Trevor is because you've been brainwashed into thinking like that. But don't worry – Dr. Klüver can easily undo the damage.'

'No!' she cried, shrinking away from me. 'I don't trust him. I don't trust any of you. You're all against Trevor! I'm going to wait in my bedroom until he arrives.'

She ran out of the door.

'There must be something we can do,' said Mo, after a pause. 'We can't let her go through life thinking that bastard is some kind of saint.'

'I can't force her into anything,' pointed out Klüver. 'If she refuses treatment I'm powerless.'

I hit my forehead in a gesture of self-reproach. 'This has been badly mishandled. We should have gone along with whatever she said at first – to gain her trust. Then she might have agreed to be treated. As it is we've alienated her completely.'

Klüver nodded his agreement.

'Those tape-recordings really do exist, I suppose?' I asked him.

'Of course.'

'Then at least Paxton should be convicted. That's one small mercy.'

And so it proved to be. The jury required little deliberation to find Trevor Ralph Paxton guilty of murdering Owen Phillimore.

Lucy refused to take any part in the trial, and to this day believes her husband is the victim of a terrible miscarriage of justice. She visits him regularly in prison, and has stubbornly refused any kind of psychiatric help, from Klüver or anyone else.

A number of articles appeared in the serious press about her unusual situation. It became something of a *cause célèbre* for a while. One Labour M.P. even called for the total abolition of hypnosis.

I was most impressed, however, by a thought-provoking piece in the *Guardian*. It expressed doubts as to whether Paxton could ever have found contentment with his wife, knowing that 'every word of devotion she spoke was artificial, every embrace a synthetic sham.' It concluded: 'To believe that love can exist without free will – that, surely, is the biggest self-delusion of all.'

Within the last month there has been a concerted campaign to persuade Paxton to confess everything from prison, in the hope that this will make Lucy more amenable to a course of de-programming. It remains to be seen whether he bows to public pressure and does the right thing.

GARDENER'S QUESTIONS

CHAPTER ONE

As a general rule I avoid my namesake's meretricious habit of drawing multiple inferences from a casual glance at a person. But in the case of Mr. George Beaumaris, who visited our consulting-parlour one afternoon in the late spring of 2013, I was tempted to make a rare exception.

'Let me hazard that you are retired, or perhaps of private means. You possess two or more cars, at least one of which is a vintage model. As to hobbies, you are an enthusiastic, not to say a fanatical gardener.'

My visitor grinned broadly, which had the effect of inverting his foxy brown moustache.

'You certainly live up to your name,' he said, 'I *am* a keen gardener. How could you tell?'

'Your clothes are impeccably tailored, yet there are splashes of fresh mud on your shoes and trousers, and what I take to be earth underneath your fingernails. Obviously you felt compelled to tend your beloved plants despite this morning's torrential rain. It even made you half an hour late for our appointment.'

'Ah, yes, sorry about that,' said Beaumaris, shifting in his seat. 'I'm afraid my rosarium has become a bit of an obsession over the years. You ought to see it, Mr. Webster, next time you're in the Saffron Walden area.'

'Thank you, I will. But what about my other conjectures? Was I right about the cars?'

'Yes. I own four in all; three from the thirties, and that Volvo estate outside. It was the R.A.C. Club tie that gave me away, I suppose?'

'Quite. And are you retired?'

'Have been since my father died, twelve years ago. I was lucky enough to inherit a considerable estate.'

'Which explains how you managed to see me at such short notice. A man with professional commitments would surely have needed longer. But I'm digressing from the purpose of your visit, Mr. Beaumaris. A problem concerning your new fiancée, if I remember correctly?'

'Yes. I think it's off beat enough for you. Let me put the thing into context first, if I may. My wife, Gloria, died in a car crash two years ago. She was driving back from my sister's house when she lost control of the car. We'd been happily married for many years.'

'Very distressing,' I sympathised.

Beaumaris nodded, his eyes moistening slightly.

'Yes – yes it was. Still haven't really got over it, to be honest. Anyway, last year a close friend suggested I should try to meet some other women. He said it would be therapeutic – bring me out of myself. At first I was reluctant, but my friend persisted, and in the end I agreed to join a dating agency – Top Table Introductions.'

'Sounds rather exclusive,' I commented.

'Well, I suppose it was, in a way. They put me in touch with several suitable ladies, some of whom were extremely charming, others less so. But there was no *spark* with any of them, if you know what I mean. I quickly became disillusioned – told the agency not to bother with me any more. Several months passed, and I'd completely forgotten about the whole thing when I got a call from a woman named Janine Yorke. She'd been given my details by the agency at the same time as the others, but hadn't got round to phoning me till then. I imagine she was just as sceptical about the process as I was. We got chatting, and she seemed to be on my wave length, so I decided to give it one last go.

'We met for lunch the next day, at a country hotel just outside St. Albans. It transpired that she shared my passion for flowers. I was pleasantly surprised, because none of the other ladies I'd met were particularly interested. In fact Janine fulfilled virtually all the requirements I put on my original application form. Even down to the auburn hair!'

'Can you still remember what those requirements were?'

'Yes, I think so. Honesty – that was at the top of my list, beauty, good sense of humour, height between five foot three and five foot seven, age between thirty-five and fifty. The red hair and love of gardening were optional extras, really. Oh, and I don't like spectacles on a woman.'

'How old is Janine?'

'She's thirty-six.'

'I see. Please continue.'

'Well, things went pretty smoothly after that first meeting. She came to my house the following weekend. I showed her round the garden, and she rattled off the names of some of the plants, in Latin. I suppose that's when I really fell for her. Within a month we were engaged.'

'This all sounds most heart-warming,' I said. 'But presumably something went awry otherwise you wouldn't be here?'

Beaumaris nodded gloomily. 'We fixed a date for the wedding. Then I decided I ought to tell Top Table about their successful match. However, Janine had heard rumours that the agency had gone bust recently, which was a bit sad. I phoned their number, and sure enough it was unobtainable. I did some research – unbeknownst to Janine – and tracked down the proprietress Mary Catchpole. She was the one who originally conducted my personality assessment.'

'Why unbeknownst to Janine?'

'I had the vague idea of inviting Miss Catchpole to our wedding, as a surprise.'

'I see. Go on.'

'I phoned her at home, and she confirmed that her business had indeed gone under. I offered my commiserations. Then I told her the good news about Janine and me, and thanked her sincerely for bringing us together. She seemed a little overwhelmed at first – didn't know what to say. After a long pause she congratulated me on my choice of partner. I asked her if she'd like to come to the wedding, and she said she'd be honoured.'

'This still seems very positive, Mr. Beaumaris,' I objected. 'When do we get to the problem?'

He held up his hand.

'Soon. You see, when Janine heard I'd contacted Mary Catchpole she became upset.'

'Why?'

'She said she was embarrassed about needing to use a dating agency at all. It was a stigma – something she wanted to forget about.'

'Well, that's understandable.'

'I suppose so. Anyway, we agreed that in future if anyone asked where we met we'd say at a party. I thought that would satisfy her.'

'And did it?'

'To an extent. But from then on she seemed to change.'

'In what way?'

'She became nervy, moody. And she started asking me for money.'

'Ah!' I said, knowingly.

'You're thinking "gold-digger", I suppose?' said Beaumaris, stiffening.

'It's something to be considered,' I replied, as gently as I could. 'After all, you're a rich man, and she's somewhat younger than you.'

'But the point is I'd already arranged that she should receive an annual allowance of forty thousand pounds after marriage.'

'Really? She knew about this?'

'Yes.'

'Janine has no resources of her own?'

'Nothing to speak of.'

'But what did she need money for – so urgently that it couldn't wait until after the wedding?'

'Her nose.'

'Her nose?' I repeated, rather taken aback.

'That's right. She said it was too long, and that she wouldn't feel confident enough to go through with the wedding unless she had cosmetic surgery.'

Beaumaris plunged a hand into his breast pocket and drew out a photograph.

'This is Janine – taken before I met her. Do you see anything wrong with her nose? I'm damned if I can.'

I took a good look, before agreeing that it seemed perfectly acceptable.

'Of course, a profile shot would be more useful,' I remarked.

'She's adorable from every angle – believe me.'

I shrugged. 'Women can be irrational when it comes to their own appearance, Mr. Beaumaris.'

'You may be right. In any case I gave her a cheque for twenty thousand pounds, on the understanding that it was an advance against her first year's allowance.'

'And how much did the surgery cost?'

'Let's just say there wasn't any change.'

'Well, I hope it was a success!'

'She seemed pleased enough. But, between you and me, I couldn't see much difference afterwards. And, if that wasn't enough, last week she asked me for more money – to buy clothes. "I need a new wardrobe to go with my new face", she said.'

'How much did she ask for?'

'Ten thousand.'

I blew out my cheeks. 'That much?'

'Yes, she wanted "designer labels."'

Beaumaris folded his freckled hands and leant over the desk earnestly. He looked like a sad fox.

'Please understand, I'm not worried about the money, Mr. Webster. But I am concerned about Janine. Do you think she's mentally unstable?'

I turned and gazed down thoughtfully at the Crawford Street traffic.

'Difficult for me to give an opinion off the cuff. This sudden burst of prodigality is certainly singular, even eccentric. But whether it amounts to anything clinical is another matter. Would you say she is acting out of character at the moment?'

'Yes, definitely. The girl I fell in love with was fun loving, stable, selfless – someone I wanted to spend the rest of my life with.'

'But the person she's become?'

He shook his head forlornly. 'I don't know. Perhaps I should postpone the wedding plans?'

143

'That is something only you can decide, I'm afraid.'

Beaumaris slumped in his seat, disappointed that I was unable to provide an instant solution.

'It might help if I knew something of Janine's background,' I suggested after a pause. 'What about her family?'

'Parents live in Lincolnshire. Janine's never really got on with them – they hardly ever speak. She has a younger brother, Toby. I met him once – seems affable enough. He's a sculptor.'

'Successful?'

'Not yet. I bought one of his sculptures – he calls them "machines".'

'How about her friends?'

'I get the feeling she's keeping them away from me.'

'What makes you say that?'

'Well, I've only met one since we met, and that was by accident. She's called Fatima – Turkish, I think. I called round to Janine's flat one afternoon and she happened to be there.'

'What's she like?'

'Don't really know. By the time I came in she'd already disappeared into the bedroom. She's in Purdah – not allowed to show herself to men without wearing a veil.'

'Ah, I see.'

After some reflection I said: 'You know, I'm going to have to talk to Janine at length before I can give an opinion on this matter.'

'Of course. The trouble is I don't want her knowing I've hired a detective. I feel guilty enough about it as it is.'

'That might be a problem.'

'I've already given it some thought,' announced Beaumaris with a surge of enthusiasm, 'and I think I've got a solution. You could come to my house on the pretext of

investigating a burglary. I own a number of Art Deco figurines – several thousand pounds worth, in fact. I'll hide
them away somewhere, and say they've been stolen. That way
you could ask anything you want without arousing Janine's
suspicions. Does it make any sense?'

'Y-es,' I replied hesitantly, 'I suppose it could work.'

'Good!' exclaimed my visitor with satisfaction.

'But I'd like to bring along my partner, Mr. Rennie, if
you have no objections. He'll be properly briefed before-
hand, of course. Would this weekend suit you?'

'Perfect. I'll make sure Janine's around. And I'll invite
my sister along, to create a more natural atmosphere.'

And so it was that on a bright, blowy Saturday morning
Morris and I found ourselves heading up the M11 on a
covert mission. The journey was a dull and featureless one,
and by the time we neared our exit my associate had nodded off in the passenger seat.

'We're nearly there,' I said, giving him a nudge. 'Now,
are you completely happy with the cover story?'

'I think so,' he replied, stretching his long limbs and
yawning. 'We've been hired to trace some Art Deco figurines. But I still think it's a dud case. A neurotic woman
who spends too much money and worries about her looks!
Where's the mileage in that?'

'Ah, but what has caused Janine's recent transformation
of character? That is the fascinating question. I believe this
case could just turn out to be a little gem.'

'Well, I hope you're right,' muttered Mo, who had been
in a peculiarly negative frame of mind all morning.

I noticed he had withdrawn what looked like a theatre
ticket from his jacket pocket, and was staring at it in an intense
manner. Suddenly he tore it up with a snort of disgust.

'Why did you do that?' I asked.

'It was for tonight. I was supposed to be taking Anita.'

'Why didn't you say, for God's sake? I would have come on my own.'

Mo shook his head. 'You told me you needed my help. That was more important.'

'Who is Anita, anyway? Have I met her?'

'No, and I doubt you ever will, now. She wasn't at all pleased about being put off.'

Mo's long, slightly unshaven chin seemed to be touching his knees.

'Read the map – it will take your mind off things,' I suggested cheerily.

We left the motorway at Junction 9 and doubled back on ourselves. Then we wound through the elegant little town of Saffron Walden – famously founded on the spice, and still showing evidence of former civic pride and affluence. Three or four miles further east was a long, sprawling village where the houses were all colour-washed in a pleasing variety of pastel shades, so typical of the region. At the farthest end was a large thatched farmhouse, set apart in its own considerable gardens. A yew-flanked drive brought us to the front door. I parked next to a scruffy-looking Citroen 2CV.

Soon an upright lady with snow white hair stepped out onto the gravel.

'Welcome, gentlemen,' she began, with a serene smile. 'I'm afraid my brother's been held up. He's at the garden centre – again. Choosing umbrella frames for his weeping standards.'

We were led, somewhat mystified by the jargon, straight into the dining room. A salad lunch had been prepared.

'Please, help yourself, gentlemen. George specifically asked us not to wait. He shouldn't be too long now. Oh, this is my husband, Lars.'

A diffident, craggy-faced old man rose from his seat and shook our hands rather automatically. He had dim, watery blue eyes, and gave the impression of being extremely tired of life.

'You are security experts?' he enquired of Mo, in a Scandinavian accent.

'Well, yes, we're here about the missing figurines.'

'Good.'

With that monosyllable Lars retreated into sullen silence – obviously his preferred state. He chomped on his food like a cow.

'You may want to take a look at the drawing room after lunch,' Daphne suggested helpfully. 'There are some nice things in there – good silver, and porcelain. I've been telling my brother for years that he needs to be more careful about security. The world is a wicked place these days, isn't it?'

'How right you are,' I agreed solemnly.

'It really makes my blood boil when I think of those lovely little figurines,' she continued. 'They had great sentimental value for George, you know. He gave them to Gloria – his late wife – on her fortieth birthday. I didn't even realize they'd been stolen until yesterday. My brother keeps everything important to himself. Always has.' She laughed to herself. 'I only found out he was engaged from our family solicitor, you know! Ah, this looks like him now.'

We broke off eating to peer out of the window. Beaumaris's Volvo swept past us and headed for the garage. Minutes later the man himself walked into the dining room arm-in-arm with his fiancée.

'Ah, good, I see you've started without me. Hello, Mr. Webster, Mr. Rennie. I appreciate you both driving up at the weekend. This is Janine, by the way.'

Miss Yorke acknowledged us with a lightening-quick smile. She had a delicate, pleasing face, with full lips and dark red hair piled up in a stack. At first glance she appeared moderately tall, but I guessed that without her excessively high heels she would struggle to meet Beaumaris's minimum height requirement.

She took her place next to me and began to pick at the salad self-consciously. I studied her face. Her eyes were a little bloodshot, and every now and then her slightly pop-eyed stare would be interrupted by a flurry of blinking. That famous nose seemed perfectly in proportion, and bore no visible signs of the recent surgery.

In between courses Beaumaris cleared his throat and announced: 'Mr. Webster and his colleague will be asking us some searching questions over the next couple of days. You may think they're too personal and intrusive, and have nothing to do with the theft. But can I humbly ask you all to co-operate fully? I assure you it's all in the interests of recovering my property.'

A murmur of acquiescence went up from the gathering.

After lunch we were treated to a grand tour of the gardens, with Beaumaris acting as guide. Janine accompanied us and often chimed in – a Latin name here, a pest control tip there. Every time she made a contribution George would look at her with scarcely concealed adoration – he was clearly still besotted by her.

We came at last to the rose garden, which was a bewildering maze of stone pavements weaving through and between pergolas, pillars, arches and trelisses. It must have covered an acre at least.

'Unfortunately we're a little early for most of the varieties. But not this one. *This* is my absolute pride and joy.'

Beaumaris was pointing to a bush that could already boast a proliferation of glossy, well-packed blooms in a delicate pink.

'Gloria's Choice. That's the official name.'

'In honour of your late wife?' I asked.

'Yes. It's a hybrid of *wichuraiana*. Took me years to breed. Painstaking business, you know.'

'The scent is out of this world,' enthused Janine, stooping down and holding a flower to her nostrils. 'I hope you'll name one after *me* one day, George,' she added pointedly.

'Of course I will,' replied Beaumaris, patting her on the head.

I could not help but notice Janine's hair darkened near the roots.

'Mr. Rennie, you asked to see the Hybrid Teas, didn't you? They're over this side – let me show you,' offered Beaumaris, strategically steering Mo away. 'Darling, could you take Mr. Webster through to the wild roses? You know as much about them as I do. We'll meet you back at the house a bit later.'

This was clearly a stage-managed opportunity for me to quiz Janine in private.

She led me through an ornamental iron gate, into a less structured section of the garden. It consisted of rose bushes which had been left pretty much to their own devices.

'Well, have you got any theories yet?' she asked, cocking her head at me challengingly.

'About the figurines?'

'What else?'

'Actually, we believe the burglars had inside information. Someone close to Mr. Beaumaris may have talked to an outsider – tipped them off unwittingly. That's how the thieves knew the lay-out of the house, and exactly where to find the valuable items.'

Janine considered this in silence, pausing to inspect a broken branch.

'Your fiancé is a very wealthy man, Miss Yorke. In my experience money tends to attract trouble. It's inevitable, I'm afraid.'

'So, how can I help?'

'I need to know if you've discussed this house with anyone – friends, relations, anybody at all. Think carefully. What about your parents?'

Janine gave me an icy stare.

'We haven't spoken for months.'

'They know you're engaged to George, presumably?'

'No, not yet. I'll have to tell them eventually, I suppose.'

'What about brothers or sisters?'

'I've got a brother. He's visited the house once.'

'Really?'

'But Toby's completely trustworthy. Certainly not a criminal.'

'I'm sure you're right. All the same it might be worth speaking to him. He may have been indiscreet without realizing it.'

She shrugged. 'Go and talk to him if you want. He's very busy, though, I warn you.'

I paused, and steeled myself before asking: 'Is it true that you and George met through a dating agency?'

Janine's chin went up indignantly.

'Who told you?'

'Well, he did, as a matter of fact.'

'Am I allowed no privacy?'

'I'm sorry, but we do have to cover everything. This is all in the strictest confidence, I assure you of that.' My emollient tone hardly seemed to pacify her, but I pushed on with the line of enquiry anyway. 'Did any of the other men you dated seem suspicious in any way?'

Janine looked blank. 'No, not particularly.'

'You haven't got their contact details still, by any chance?'

'Of course I haven't. What a ridiculous idea!'

'Can you remember anything about them that might help?'

'It was a long time ago, Mr. Webster,' she replied impatiently. 'Is this relevant to the figurines?'

'It could be. Anything could be.'

'Well, I'm afraid I can't help you. Meeting George has blocked out my recollection of the other people completely.'

'Yes,' I agreed, with a sentimental smile, 'that's what love does, I suppose. Never fear, I can always look up what I need to know in the agency files.'

'Aren't they meant to be confidential?'

'There are ways and means, Miss Yorke, in this computer age. You'd be surprised how easily one can access such information. It's shocking, really, but it's all part of my job.'

Suddenly Janine stopped dead in her tracks and exclaimed: 'I've got it!'

'What?'

'My brother, Toby, mentioned some chap he'd met who was very interested in George's antiques. What an idiot! Why didn't I think of it before?'

'Who was this person?'

'I don't know – one of Toby's boozing acquaintances. He wanted to know all about the architecture of the house. Claimed to be into Art Deco stuff. Toby was a bit suspicious of him at the time.'

'Well,' I reacted, rather thrown off guard, 'this could be the breakthrough we've been looking for. Thank you, Miss Yorke.'

'I presume you'll want to speak to Toby about it as soon as possible? I'll try and arrange it.'

'Oh, the sooner the better.'

Janine looked at me very earnestly, her eyelids twitching madly. 'Do you think this man could turn out to be the thief?'

'It's a distinct possibility. In fact, we ought to find Mr. Beaumaris and give him the good news straightaway!'

Beaumaris found it hard to know how he should react. He leant against the mantelpiece in the drawing room with brows drawn, puffing nervously on a cigarette.

'You're quite sure this person was interested in Art Deco, specifically?' he asked Janine, who was perching eagerly on the end of the sofa.

'That's what Toby said. You could look a bit more pleased, George. I've probably identified the thief for you!'

He gave an awkward smile. 'I'm delighted, of course, darling. I just want to get the details absolutely straight.'

'Get Toby to tell you the whole story himself. You'll have to wait a couple of days, though – he's up in Bradford at the moment.'

'In the meantime,' I put in, giving Beaumaris a meaningful glance, 'Mr. Rennie and I should look over the house, in case the burglar left any clues. We'll review your security arrangements at the same time.'

'Let me know if you need me,' said Beaumaris, stubbing out his cigarette. 'I'll be in the study.'

We got to work immediately. Mo took the ground floor, whilst I took the first. The hunt for clues was entirely bogus, of course, but it had to be performed for appearance's sake. After an hour or so I rejoined my colleague, and together we ventured into the grounds.

❧ ❧ ❧

As soon as we were clear of the house Mo grabbed my arm.

'What's going on, Sherl? Who is this guy who's supposed to have stolen the figurines? We've got a prime suspect for a crime that never happened!'

'Well said, Mo. That is exactly what we have. It's our misfortune that someone just happened to enquire about them. Perhaps I should have foreseen something like this, and planned for it.'

'You can't cover every eventuality,' replied Mo, understandingly. 'But do we really have to pretend we're investigating the man?'

'It would look pretty odd if we didn't.'

Mo conceded the point with a thoughtful nod. 'And what about Janine? Have you found out why she's been behaving eccentrically? That's why we're here, isn't it?'

'Not much to report, as yet,' I admitted.

Mo drew me nearer, and lowered his voice confidentially. 'I managed to get some juicy gossip out of Mrs. Dando, the cook, while you were upstairs.'

'Oh yes?' I reacted, happy that Mo was taking a positive approach.

'Yes, she was being very indiscreet – a bit tipsy, I think. Apparently George's sister, Daphne, got a decent share of their father's inheritance. She was worth quite a bit. That was until talkative Lars convinced her to invest in a hairbrained scheme in Denmark. She lost it all. Ever since then they've survived on handouts from brother George.'

'Mm. That is interesting.'

'And there's something else. You see that small lake, on the other side of the orchard? Janine had a boating accident there not so long ago. Did you know that?'

'No.'

'She took out a leaky rowing boat, and nearly drowned. According to Mrs. Dando, Daphne knew it was dangerous – but failed to warn Janine.'

'I see. Where was Beaumaris during all this?'

'In Saffron Walden, seeing his dentist.'

Reading my friend's features I could tell he had a theory and was itching to expound it.

'What is your conclusion?' I asked.

'Obviously Daphne wants to get rid of Janine.'

'Why?'

'Well, at the moment she has a chance of inheriting her brother's money when he dies. But if he marries he's bound to leave virtually everything to his new wife. That's a good enough motive, I would have thought.'

'Why should Daphne expect to outlive her brother? She looks quite a bit older than him.'

'Perhaps she intends *to make sure he dies first.*'

'Murder?'

'Why not?' said Mo with widening eyes. 'I think she probably caused Beaumaris's first wife to have that fatal accident – tampered with her car.'

'We seem to be heaping surmise upon surmise, here. In any case, I'm not sure your theory can explain Janine's sudden vanity, or her desire to spend money like water.'

Mo drew up his wide shoulders. 'I'll have to work on that.'

Over supper I had a chance to make a re-examination of Daphne and Lars in the light of Mo's fresh intelligence. Was it my imagination, or did I sense an antagonism towards Janine – this would-be interloper? It manifested in nothing more than an over-politeness, perhaps an unguarded facial expression – signals that could easily be misinterpreted, or overlooked entirely.

After the meal Beaumaris suggested bridge, and we all shuffled off to the drawing room.

I partnered our host, whilst Daphne partnered her husband. Janine was an interested observer, and Mo – not much of a bridge player at the best of times – read a magazine by the light of a standard lamp.

As the first few hands were played we could hear the wind working itself up almost into a gale; there was a constant melancholy whine as it blew down through the huge old chimney. After about an hour Daphne, who was dummy at the time, yawned showily.

'Would you like us to call it a night?' George asked her kindly. 'You look done in.'

'I am wilting a little,' she admitted, rubbing her eyes. 'But I don't want to spoil the game for everyone else.'

'Janine can take your place, can't you, darling?'

'Of course,' replied George's fiancée brightly. 'I'm still not very good, though, so you'll have to make allowances.'

Daphne got up and kissed her husband lightly on the top of his broad head.

'I shall make myself a milk drink before turning in,' she announced, sweeping regally out of the room.

We played out the hand, and I was in the process of totting up the scores, when there was a gut-wrenching scream from somewhere in the house.

'What the hell's that?' exclaimed Beaumaris, jumping up.

'Sounds like Daphne,' said Janine, her eyelids going into another nervous spasm.

Lars, who had done more than justice to a bottle of port, hardly stirred from his chair, but the rest of us hurried towards the source of the noise. We met Daphne running back along the hall. She was deadly pale – there was no more colour in her cheeks than in her snowy hair.

'What is it? What's happened?' demanded Beaumaris, grabbing his sister by the shoulder.

She was gulping, like a fish out of water, unable to speak for several seconds. Finally she managed to blurt out: 'Eyes! At the window!'

'Where?'

'In the kitchen. It was horrible! Just eyes – nothing else. No face.'

'Perhaps it was a ghost?' theorized Janine darkly. 'I always said this house was haunted.'

'Come on,' said Beaumaris authoritatively, signalling to Mo and me. 'There could be an intruder. Let's take a look.'

We made a thorough search of the kitchen, the pantry, and the boiler room, before stepping out onto the terrace and peering into the night.

'She must have been hallucinating,' muttered our client. 'There's nothing out here.'

We returned to the drawing room to find Daphne huddled on the sofa, trembling, and being comforted by Janine.

'Are you quite sure about this, Daphne?' asked Beaumaris. 'Could it not have been a reflection, or a trick of the light?'

She shook her head vehemently. 'No, somebody was out there, George, I swear. But only the eyes – no face. Didn't you find anything?'

'Not a sausage. Whoever it was obviously got scared and ran off into the garden.'

'I won't be able to sleep tonight,' she warned, 'or tomorrow night. Not until I know who it was, and what they wanted.'

Beaumaris let out a resigned sigh. 'Shall we make a search of the grounds? Would that put your mind at ease?'

'Not much point, if it is a ghost,' objected Janine. 'I believe in them, personally.'

A rather discursive debate on spiritual matters followed, after which it was decided that Mo, Beaumaris and myself should do a quick inspection of the garden using torches, just to be on the safe side.

It was a moonless night, and the buffeting north wind was uncomfortably chilly. We fanned out across the grass, the lights from the house helping us on our way. Once beyond their influence, however, we were completely reliant on the narrow beams of our torches.

I ended up in what I presumed was the rose garden. In the dark the arched pathways took on a decidedly eerie aspect, and I was rather glad to emerge at the other side, onto the expanse of the croquet lawn. Striking out across it I heard the roar of a car engine up ahead.

'This way!' I yelled to the others, making towards the sound. Two red rear-lights became visible through the trees, receding rapidly towards the road, and then disappearing into the village.

'Was that car in our drive?' asked Beaumaris, running up to join me.

'Yes, I'm pretty sure it was.'

'So, there really was an intruder,' panted Mo, who was a few yards behind us.

We trudged back to the house in silence, disappointed at having only partially resolved the mystery.

Janine's svelte figure was silhouetted in the doorway.

'Did you see anything?' she asked eagerly, stepping out to meet us.

'Well, it wasn't a ghost – unless they drive cars these days,' responded Beaumaris dryly.

Janine looked rather put out. She obviously relished the idea of a ghostly visitor.

CHAPTER TWO

The following morning Mo and I decided to return to London. It seemed that we were in danger of getting completely bogged down in a series of inexplicable events, and I wanted to take stock of things. Beaumaris was not too happy about the idea.

'I really think you might have stayed on, Mr. Webster,' he grumbled, seeing us to our car. 'At least until you gave me a preliminary opinion.' Lowering his voice to a whisper he added: 'Time is running out. I need to know whether to cancel all the wedding arrangements. The guests have to be warned well in advance.'

'Of course, I appreciate your predicament. Give me a ring this afternoon at Crawford Street, and we'll discuss matters further.'

As we drove off I caught a glimpse of our client in the rear-view mirror. He was gazing disconsolately after us, his moustache drooping appreciably.

'I feel rather sorry for the chap,' remarked Mo, voicing my thoughts.

In fact it was nearly ten o'clock in the evening before Beaumaris called us.

'I couldn't get away until now,' he explained.

'No need to apologise,' I remarked. 'Frankly, I wanted some time to think about the case.'

'And what have you come up with?'

'That it may be necessary to put your fiancée under surveillance for a while – just until I find an explanation for her odd behaviour.'

'You mean spy on her? No, that's quite out of the question.'

'Your scruples do you credit, but if we're to make any progress I must observe Janine in her own environment. It could make the difference between a successful outcome and no outcome.'

After a good deal of soul searching Beaumaris consented.

'Do what you have to do,' he said grudgingly. 'I've got to have some answers soon, or I'll go mad. She'll be in her flat in Hendon from Tuesday morning onwards. But for God's sake don't let her see you...'

Tuesday came, and we parked fifty yards or so from Janine's place, wearing hats and glasses for disguise. Just after eleven she emerged and walked down the hill to Hendon Central Tube station. We caught the same southbound train, changed with her at Tottenham Court Road, and followed her as she got off at Bond Street.

'Looks like another shopping expedition,' Mo whispered, as Janine stopped to eye a jeweller's window display. 'Let's hope she's not feeling too extravagant today – for George's sake. Mind you, the guy can afford it.'

She hovered outside one glitzy boutique after another, never actually entering any of them. Then she turned off into a more modest side street. There was a charity shop about halfway down, and it was into this that she finally disappeared, somewhat furtively.

After almost an hour she re-emerged, weighed down with shopping bags.

'So much for designer labels,' Mo hissed into my ear, as we followed her back onto the Tube. 'None of the stuff in there costs more than twenty quid, I should think!'

'Perhaps thirty, at the most,' I guessed.

We shadowed Janine efficiently all the way back to her flat. As soon as she was inside her front door we headed for our car.

'I think it's time to shed the disguises,' I announced.

'Then what?'

'We call on the lady, before she decides to go out again.'

'Hang on, I thought this was a surveillance operation,' complained Mo.

'We've done enough surveillance for one day. Time is not on our side, and I'm desperate for solid data. I'm going to go through her belongings.'

Mo looked at me doubtfully. 'How will you manage that, while she's still in the place?'

'We're going to decoy her away for a few minutes,' I replied breezily, getting into the car and removing my bobble hat: 'You will have one of your convenient fits of cramp; just like when you're losing at tennis. Simply curl up in agony on the floor. I'll tell her that we must administer salt tablets to alleviate your suffering. There's a chemist just up the road from here. She'll toddle off to purchase said tablets, during which time I will conduct a search of the apartment. Any questions?'

'Yes. What if she asks *you* to go to the chemist?'

'I'll be busy massaging the affected muscles. Anything else?'

'What if she keeps salt tablets in the flat?'

'Then we abandon the operation.'

Before Mo could dream up further objections I led him over the road to Janine's door and pressed the bell. She appeared after a considerable delay, wearing a long black dress which still had the charity shop label attached to the sleeve.

'Oh, hello!' she exclaimed in surprise.

'Sorry to turn up unannounced like this,' I began. 'Hope you don't mind?'

'No, of course not. Why don't you come in?'

We climbed the stairs to her first-floor flat, which turned out to be very light and airy, though rather untidy.

'Sorry about the mess,' she apologised, clearing the sofa of magazines so that we could sit down. 'Is this about the figurine-snatcher? Or the ghostly intruder? Or both?'

'I have a theory that they might be one and the same person. Do you think it's possible?'

'Yes,' she replied, having weighed the idea carefully, 'I'd say it's quite likely. Criminals often return to the scene of their crime, don't they? Perhaps he left something incriminating behind, and had to come back for it? By the way, would you like some tea or coffee?'

'Let me do it,' said Mo, launching himself off the sofa. Suddenly he let out the most terrible howl and collapsed onto the carpet, clutching his calf muscle, and writhing about in apparent agony. The performance was a little over-wrought, but convincing nevertheless.

'My God!' exclaimed Janine, horrified, 'What's the matter?'

'Salt tablets – it's cramp!' I cried, kneeling beside him. 'Have you got any?'

She shook her head.

'Is there a chemist nearby?'

'Yes, five minutes away. You want me to get them?'

'Would you mind? I'll try some emergency massage.'

Janine gathered up her handbag and was out of the door at top speed.

I ran to the window, and made sure she was out of sight, before going into the bedroom and beginning my search.

Several of the shopping bags from the charity shop had been hurriedly stuffed into a wardrobe. As to Janine's other clothes, some of them may have looked expensive at first; but as they had no common manufacturer or style I suspected they were second-hand also.

Under the bed was a pile of books; most were on the subject of gardening. *Know Your Roses,* a large pictorial volume, caught my eye in particular. It was in good condition – a recent purchase. Others were from the local library; again, recently borrowed. There were more books displayed on a shelf in the living room, but none of these were gardening books.

I was just about to go through some correspondence when Mo shouted out a warning.

'You've got about thirty seconds, Sherl, she's coming down the street!'

I swiftly returned everything to its place. Then we resumed our theatricals on the carpet.

A few moments later Janine burst through the door, out of breath, and brandishing a small package.

'Salt tablets!' she gasped.

'Wonderful!' I replied. 'All we need now is water.'

'Right.'

She hurried into the kitchen and returned with a glassful.

The medication was administered, and within five minutes Mo had made an impressive recovery.

'I'm OK now,' he assured, walking gingerly from one side of the room to the other. 'I don't know what I'd have done without you, Miss Yorke!'

'Don't mention it,' she answered with a laugh. 'I'm just amazed those tablets work so quickly,' she added unsuspiciously. 'Now, why don't I make that coffee? After that we could go and see my brother. That is, if you're feeling up to it?'

'I'll be up to it,' replied Mo, shooting a glance in my direction. 'Where does he live?'

'Quite near – Muswell Hill.'

Toby Yorke, a long-haired, elongated version of Janine, lived above a newsagent. His 'studio' turned out to be little more than a sparsely furnished one-bedroom flat. It was given over completely to the creation of abstract sculpture, much of which seemed to consist of everyday items covered in cotton-wool.

'I'm afraid I can't stop,' he warned, a little gruffly, as we trooped in.

An ironing-board was being given the cotton-wool treatment at that very moment.

'Do you actually sell these things?' asked Mo, tactlessly.

'Now and then,' he replied, between clenched teeth.

'Tell them about the man in the pub, Toby,' ordered Janine, settling down on a large floor-cushion. 'The whole story.'

The sculptor finished what he was doing, rubbed his hands on a towel, then condescended to give us his full attention.

'I met this bloke called Albert, in the Marlborough Arms – it was a couple of weeks ago now. He was *extremely* interested in George's Art Deco collection.'

'Albert who?' I asked.

'I don't think he ever mentioned his surname.'

'And what kind of man was he?'

Toby lit a cigarette and pondered. 'Pretty dodgy, to be honest. I'd seen him in the Marlborough once before. He told me he'd recently come out of the army. But with hindsight it's more likely he was doing time!'

'Did you give him any information?'

'Yes, unfortunately I was on the strong stuff that evening. I told him about the figurines. He kept asking whether George would sell. I said I thought it was highly unlikely. Then he wanted to know about the architecture of the house. That's when I got a bit suspicious.'

'How did the conversation end?'

'He left, suddenly – without finishing his drink, I seem to remember. Haven't seen him since.'

Janine looked at me expectantly. 'Well? What do you think?'

'I think he's our man alright,' I declared.

A few hours later we made our way over to the Marlborough Arms, on the off chance that this Albert would turn up again. Janine and her brother were both especially keen on the idea, and I could think of no legitimate reason to object.

By ten o'clock it was becoming obvious that our man was not going to put in an appearance, which was a blessing. I didn't really fancy having to interrogate him about a non-existent theft! However, the evening was far from being uneventful.

We were just debating whether Albert might frequent one of the other pubs in the Muswell Hill area. Toby, Janine, and myself were facing the bar, but Mo, sitting opposite, could look out onto the street through the bay window. The curtains were not drawn, even though it was nearly dark.

During a lull in our conversation I noticed Mo's attention had been drawn to something outside. His eyes grew round with fear, his lean jaw dropped, and the colour drained from his face.

'Did you see that?' he exclaimed, pointing over my shoulder.

'What?' we all asked.

'That face, at the window.'

We turned round. There was nothing.

'Was it another ghost?' suggested Janine excitedly.

Mo didn't answer. I could tell he was genuinely shaken by what he'd seen.

'What did it look like?' I asked.

'Just a pair of eyes – like Daphne saw that night,' he murmured. 'A woman's eyes.'

I got up from the table and headed for the door.

Toby drained his glass and hurried after me. 'Wait – I'll come with you.'

Stepping out onto the quiet street we heard rapid footsteps – someone was running away down a side alley. We sprinted off in pursuit. Toby easily outran me, and emerged onto a main road.

'Too late!' he declared, as I caught him up. 'We've lost her in the crowd.'

'No, over there!' I shouted, pointing to a woman in flowing black garb who was dashing for a West End-bound bus on the other side of the street. She managed to jump onto it through a feat of athleticism. I looked around for a free taxi in which to continue the chase, but by the time one came along the bus was miles away.

❧ ❧ ❧

The next morning Mo rolled into the Crawford Street office an hour later than arranged. He appeared pale and drawn, and had dark rings under his eyes.

'You don't look as if you've had much sleep,' I observed solicitously.

'No, hardly any,' he mumbled, slumping down on the sofa. 'I'm absolutely knackered. Kept thinking about that face at the window.'

'Never mind; we might be near to a solution of the mystery.'

'Really? What's happened?'

'Quite a lot. For a start I had a call from our esteemed and long-suffering client early this morning. He wants us off the case.'

'Great!'

'As we've discovered nothing sinister about Janine he's decided that she's worth a risk. The marriage goes ahead as planned.'

Mo shrugged. 'That's that, I suppose.'

'However,' I continued, adjusting the pipe-rack in front of me, 'since then I've reviewed the salient facts, and come up with a theory which explains them. It's a largely uncorroborated theory, and it entails putting two and two together to make five. But I am forced by circumstance to show my hand prematurely.'

'In other words, it's a guess,' said Mo penetratingly. 'Go on then, hit me with it.'

'The whole thing revolves around Fatima, Janine's muslim school friend – the one that Beaumaris encountered by accident. I believe – and this is a guess – that she suffers from an unsightly facial disfigurement which must be coverered up at all times. Recently Fatima came to Janine asking for financial help, in order to pay for expensive cosmetic surgery. Being a sympathetic and resourceful girl, Janine found a way to raise the money for her old friend. She pretended to Beaumaris that she wanted a nose job for herself.'

'Which she never had?'

'No, nor did she buy that wardrobe of expensive clothes. She bought second hand stuff that could *pass* as haute couture. Beaumaris's money went straight towards Fatima's medical expenses.'

'Do you think it could have been Fatima that I saw at the pub window?'

I nodded. 'And Fatima that Daphne spotted outside Beaumaris's kitchen. She was wearing a veil; not for religious reasons, but because the operation was only a partial success. The face was masked out, leaving only the eyes visible.'

'But what the hell was she doing, peering at us through windows?'

'Perhaps she wanted to speak to Janine, but couldn't build up the courage to come inside and face the rest of us.'

Mo took a few seconds to digest all this, and then asked: 'Why don't you put your theory to Beaumaris – see what he says? It can't do any harm.'

'Already have,' I replied with a quick smile. 'In fact I'd just come off the phone to him when you walked in.'

'How did he react?'

'Surprisingly well, actually. He said that if I was right he would admire Janine even more, because of her heartening compassion for a friend's suffering. He's going to put the whole thing to her when he sees her this afternoon, and then report back to me.'

'Good – we're making progress,' said my colleague, stretching his legs out. 'Now, if you have no objections I'm going to get some kip. Wake me up when he calls.'

Ominously, there was no news from Beaumaris for two days. Then we received a letter from him which ran this way:

Dear Mr. Webster,

You may be pleased to learn that Janine has confirmed your theory in virtually every particular! A few years ago her schoolfriend (who is neither Turkish nor called Fatima, by the way) had an accident with a home tanning device, which left her scarred on the face. There was a lengthy waiting list for corrective surgery on the N.H.S.

The friend, hearing that Janine was engaged to a wealthy man, approached her for help. The rest, as they say, is history.

My only regret in all this is that my fiancée took such a dim view of my character, and assumed that I would be unwilling to finance the operation, which, I hear, has been 90% successful. I trust she will get to know me rather better after we are married. By the way, the schoolfriend has asked to remain incognito, at least until she feels able to confront the world again.

I enclose a cheque, and two invitations to the wedding, as a small token of my heart-felt gratitude.

Hope to see you both soon.

Yours sincerely,
George Beaumaris.

'I'm going to frame this and stick it up on the wall – there, next to dear old Queen Victoria,' declared Mo, waving aside my protestations. 'No false modesty, Sherl. It will be a permanent reminder that two and two make five.'

CHAPTER THREE

The wedding ceremony was a quiet registry-office affair in Saffron Walden, blessed by lovely June sunshine. Beaumaris had invited a number of long-standing friends, as well as some extended family. Only Toby attended from Janine's side, however, which gave the whole event an unbalanced feel. Presumably Mr. and Mrs. Yorke objected to their daughter's match so strongly that they felt compelled to stay away.

There were two other notable absentees: the disfigured schoolfriend, and Mary Catchpole, managing director of the now defunct Top Table Introductions.

The bride looked suitably radiant, dressed in a pale pink lace-edged confection, while the groom was dapper, self-conscious, and fidgety.

The reception was held back at Beaumaris's house. A string quartet played on the lawn, and there was a marquee serving lavish refreshments. Lars, who had the honour of being best man, made a short speech, devoid of either humour or interest.

Then Beaumaris took the microphone.

'Ladies and gentleman, thank you all for helping to make this the happiest day of my life. I have decided not to tax your patience with a lengthy peroration, but there is one thing I would like to announce: I have lied to my wife.'

There was a shocked murmur from the gathering.

'I told her that due to certain financial constraints, as well as my aversion to flying, we would be unable to go abroad for our honeymoon. She had resigned herself – without a word of complaint, I may add – to spending just one night in a seafront hotel in Brighton. However, the truth is that we are booked to go from here straight to Heathrow and thence to a luxury hotel on the Côte d'Azur. For a month!'

There was great applause, and Janine reacted with a becoming mixture of surprise and delight.

'I would like to apologise publicly for playing a practical joke on her,' continued Beaumaris, turning affectionately to his wife, 'and assure her that I don't intend to make a habit of it in the years ahead!'

More applause and laughter.

He held up a hand. 'And finally, I hope, and believe, that our married life will turn out to be a bed of roses, both metaphorically and literally. Thank you very much.'

The groom resumed his seat and kissed the bride, to an enthusiastic and sustained ovation.

Right on cue a gleaming white Rolls Royce Phantom cruised up to the house. The couple made their way to it through the euphoric crowd. As Janine settled into the back seat I thought I detected – just for a split second – a look of worry on her face.

Mo didn't notice, having been quite carried away by the festive mood.

'Cheer up, Sherl, for pity's sake!' he exclaimed, waving energetically as the car swept off towards the village. 'You're not still brooding about the case? It's over – solved. Do yourself a favour – join in with the spirit. Have another glass of bubbly.'

'I'm sorry, Mo. I was reflecting.'

'What on? Can't you just let it go?'

I smiled weakly. 'Yes, you're probably right.'

The fact was I had lost many hours of sleep in the last few weeks turning things over in my mind. Although the affair had been successfully resolved I was tormented by the notion that the solution had been too easy.

It reminded me of an exam I once took, where I finished well ahead of my class-mates. Minutes before the end I realised, to my horror, that I'd missed out a whole page of questions! It even occurred to me to resume our surveillance of Janine, without informing Beaumaris. Mo talked me out of that idea. After all, reports of Janine's recent behaviour *were* encouraging. There had been no more bizarre requests for money, or periods of uncharacteristic moodiness. In fact, she seemed to have reverted to her old self.

And yet, that strange look on her face as she was being whisked away to honeymoon bliss had reactivated all my doubts...

Just then Toby, who appeared to have overdone the champagne, lumbered towards us, glassy eyed.

'Mr. Webster, isn't it? The detective with the famous middle name? How are you, mate? Enjoying yourself?'

'Oh, absolutely. And you?'

'Too much, as you can see. But I have a bloody good excuse.'

'Yes, indeed. Your sister happily married off. It must be a relief.'

'Of course. But there's another reason. I've just got my first big commission! Bradford City Council want a bronze for their new shopping mall.'

'Congratulations.'

'Only heard about it today. Didn't even have time to tell Janine.'

'When do you start work?' enquired Mo.

'I'm going up there tonight – staying for three days. There's a lot of preparatory stuff to do before I can start. Well, I better get back to the bar. Nice to see you again. By the way, did you ever catch that thief – Albert?'

'No,' I replied, making sure I avoided Mo's amused glance. 'Unfortunately it looks like he's got away with it.'

Three days later I got a call at my flat – very early in the morning. It was George Beaumaris, and he was in quite a state.

'It's started all over again, Mr. Webster!'

'What has?' I asked, still more than half asleep.

'Janine – she's acting strangely. You did say I could call if anything went wrong.'

'Yes, of course. What exactly is she doing?'

'It started when we were driving to the airport. She remembered she'd left a window open in her flat by mistake, and asked if we could stop off there on the way. I told her it was out of the question, because we were running late and would miss our plane. She went berserk! But I put my foot down.'

'Is there anything valuable in the flat?'

'Not really. That's why I couldn't understand all the fuss. On the flight I suggested that she call Toby and ask him to pop round there and close the window. He has his own key, you see. Ever since we arrived in Nice she's been phoning him every few minutes, but he's never in. Yesterday she started ringing round his friends, but none of them knew where he was.'

'I see. What's the latest position?'

'I've just woken up to find she's left the hotel. There's a note. Shall I read it to you?'

'Please.'

' "Dear George, have decided to return to London. Back soon. Don't be cross. Love Janine." She's taken her suitcase, and two of my credit cards. I really thought we'd got over all this nonsense.'

'Let me consider the matter. Can I ring you back?'

'Alright, but don't leave it too long. I really am at my wit's end!'

I sprang out of bed, had a wash, then phoned Mo. He was rather annoyed at being disturbed so early, and thoroughly unimpressed by the latest bulletin.

'So, she's gone off her head again. What can we do about it?'

'I don't know. That's why I need your advice, Mo.'

'It's six-thirty in the morning, for God's sake,' he groaned.

'Seven-thirty in Europe. Why do you think Janine is so desperate to go to her flat? Because of one open window?'

'I haven't the faintest idea.'

'It seems like an over-reaction to me. Unless ... '

I'd just had a ghastly thought.

'Unless what?'

'No, it couldn't be ...'

'What?' repeated Mo irritably.

'Don't ask me for an explanation, Mo, but we have to get over to the flat straight away.'

'Now?'

'Yes. Right now. Get dressed and jump in a taxi. I'll meet you there.'

I hung up before my colleague could object, threw on some clothes, and shot out of the house. Luckily a cab hove into view almost immediately.

'Northolt Road, Hendon,' I instructed the driver. 'Do you know any short cuts? I'm in a great hurry.'

'I'll do my best,' he replied evenly.

'There's a tip in it for you,' I added, flourishing a ten pound note to encourage him.

We took a promising-looking back street and promptly became snagged between two off-loading lorries. It held us up for what seemed like an eternity. By the time we finally made it to Janine's place Mo was already standing outside the door, looking thoroughly bored.

'There's no answer, Sherl,' he remarked with a yawn, as I paid off the cabbie. 'She's obviously not in.'

I jammed all of the bells at once. A disgruntled man in a string vest appeared after several minutes, and began to give me a piece of his mind. I brushed past him, bounded up the stairs, and tried Janine's door. It was locked. With Mo's help we managed to kick it in.

The living room was empty, but there was orchestral music playing softly in the background.

'Someone's in,' concluded Mo.

'Not necessarily,' I retorted.

The door to the bedroom was shut.

I took a deep breath, then eased it open and peered inside.

There, amid the comparative gloom, was a woman, spread-eagled on the bed, lying quite still. She was fully clothed. Her wrists and ankles were tied to the legs of the bed, and she had masking tape stuck over her mouth. As she did not stir, even when I drew very near, I feared the worst.

'Jesus!' whispered Mo, who was just behind me. 'Who the hell's that?'

I put my ear to the woman's chest, and was relieved to hear a frail, irregular beat.

'She's alive, thank God,' I said, pulling the masking tape off.

'Help me untie her, will you.'

'But who is she?' repeated Mo.

'Her name is Mary Catchpole.'

'What! The woman who ran the dating agency?'

'Exactly. Here, look very carefully at her eyes,' I instructed, shielding the rest of her face with my hands. 'Do you recognize her? No? She's the "ghost" who gave you such a turn in the Marlborough Arms that night – the mysterious veiled woman.'

'Are you certain?'

'Absolutely,' I answered, unknotting the final cord. 'Now, we'd better ring for an ambulance.'

Once Mary Catchpole had been borne away on a stretcher I took the opportunity to continue with that unfinished search of Janine's effects.

I concentrated this time on her correspondence, and quickly came upon something useful: an envelope, addressed to her parents in Lincolnshire, which had never been posted. Through this I obtained their telephone number – from Directory Enquiries.

'Why do you want to phone Janine's parents?' asked Mo, who was beginning to sound rather lost.

'Bear with me,' I replied, dialling the number.

A man answered.

'Hello, is that Mr. Yorke?'

'Yes. Who is this?'

'Ah, my name is Webster, of Webster Rennie Associates. We're the accountants for Top Table Introductions Limited. Apparently the company owes a certain amount of back-pay to Janine Yorke, your daughter. I've been instructed to issue a cheque to her. It's not a large sum, I'm afraid – but every little helps, as they say! I am speaking to the right Mr. Yorke, aren't I?'

'Well, yes.'

'And Janine *was* employed by Top Table Introductions?'

'Yes, some time ago. She was a secretary. But I don't understand – why are you sending the money here, instead of to her own address?'

'We seem not to have a record of it, for some reason.'

'Just a moment, I'll give it to you now... yes, here we are: Flat two, number forty nine Northolt Road, Hendon. Do you want the post code?'

'No, that will be fine. Thank you, Mr. Yorke. Goodbye.'

I put the receiver down gently, and then proceeded to dance a little jig of celebration on the carpet.

'We have our solution, at long last!' I declared.

'If you say so, Sherl.'

Regaining my composure I added, in pedagogical vein: 'When all the details come to light I think we will find blackmail to be at the heart of this business. Perhaps you even suspected that yourself?'

'No,' replied Mo a little bitterly, 'I didn't. I'm not supposed to be the cerebral half of this partnership.'

I laughed. 'Quite. Well, there's no reason to reproach yourself. It's been a pretty Byzantine case, with many a blind alley. I went down one of them myself, with that theory about Fatima's facial scar.'

'Who was being blackmailed, then?'

'Janine, of course.'

'Why?'

'This is how I now read it,' I said, settling down on the sofa. 'Last year she was hired as a humble admin girl at the dating agency. At the beginning it seemed like just another temping job. But over the months she witnessed a procession of extremely wealthy, eligible men pass through the office. Some of them found a wife; the great majority did not. What a crying shame, she thought – all that net disposable income going abegging!

'Janine found she had free access to client files. At the touch of a few buttons she could discover exactly what characteristics any particular gentleman required of his dream date. This was a potential goldmine, for anyone who wanted to gold-dig.

'Her chance came when she heard the agency was about to fold. In the dying months she managed to copy information about several likely clients. Of these George Beaumaris was chosen as her main target. Why? Well, for a start he was a millionaire. Also, she fell nicely into his required age range. No doubt he gave the impression – on the one occasion when he came into the office – of being the kind of mild, middle-aged chap who would be easy to manipulate into marriage.

'But there were some obstacles to overcome. George ideally wanted a red-head who knew about roses, and who did not wear spectacles. Janine, at that time, had dark brown hair, was a botanical dunce, and *did* wear glasses.'

'How do you know that?' interrupted Mo sharply.

'Because I studied her very closely at George's house. She was wearing contact lenses which were clearly giving her trouble, as if she had only recently started using them. And when we were out in the rosarium I noticed she had hennaed hair – the darker roots were beginning to grow through. Did you ever wonder why she always had her hair up, and favoured very high heels?'

Mo shrugged.

'Because she was slightly below five foot three – Beaumaris's minimum – and had to appear taller. But all these were merely superficial changes. The hardest challenge was to pass herself off as a gardening expert. It took months of painstaking study. Look, I'll show you.'

I went off to the bedroom, and returned with a pile of books.

'*These* were her homework. All bought or borrowed suspiciously recently, you notice. Which is why they were hidden away under the bed. After three months swotting she had mastered her subject well enough to put the plan into action ...

'She telephoned Beaumaris, claiming to be just another Top Table client looking for Mr. Right. As we know, they hit it off immediately, and by the time she had demonstrated her newly-acquired botanical scholarship in Beaumaris's garden, the poor man was utterly and completely hooked! The irony is that if nothing had gone wrong they could have lived happily ever after.

'But something did go wrong. Beaumaris got it into his head to contact the M.D. of Top Table, Mary Catchpole, and tell her how he and Janine Yorke were engaged. Mary reacted with creditable self-control when she realized that one of her ex-employees must have passed herself off as a client. She decided, for the time being at least, not to give Janine away.'

'But to blackmail her instead?'

'Very perceptive, Mo. Yes, the opportunity was too tempting to pass up. Mary was also aware of how rich Beaumaris was. She wanted a slice of the cake. It was only fair ...

'One day she visited Janine at her flat and demanded a large sum in return for her silence. Janine had no choice but to comply. It would mean borrowing off Beaumaris, of course, and she needed a plausible reason. Hence the request for cosmetic surgery. Am I making sense so far?'

'So far, yes.'

'Good. Now let's jump ahead to just before the wedding. Mary turns up at Janine's flat again, in order to extort one final, huge payment. Janine knows she can't possibly raise the money, and pleads for leniency. Mary is implacable. A fight breaks out, as a result of which the blackmailer is overpowered and tied to the bed.

'Janine plans to keep Mary tied up until after the wedding, by which time she will have come into her marriage settlement, and be beyond Mary's power. However, during the reception Beaumaris springs an awkward surprise – they are to fly off to Nice immediately, for a month-long honeymoon! Obviously Mary can't be left bound and gagged for that long. She must be released, before she dies of dehydration – murder is definitely not part of the plan. Janine tells Beaumaris she wants to go to her flat, to close the window. It's a pretty feeble-sounding excuse, and her husband won't hear of making a special detour. He insists they go straight to the airport. Once in France she tries to telephone her brother, in order to elicit his help – unaware that he's in Bradford on sculpturing business.'

'Wait a minute,' Mo interrupted, 'how would she have explained the fact that there was a woman tied up on her bed?'

'No need. Toby was in on Janine's scam from the very early stages. That's my belief, anyway.'

'What makes you think that?'

'He was the only one of Janine's circle who was ever allowed to meet Beaumaris. To me that's highly significant. It suggests that Toby could be trusted not to spill the beans about her having been employed by Top Table. He *must* have known what she was up to, and probably even approved. A wealthy brother-in-law would make an excellent patron for his sculpture, after all.'

'True.'

'Anyway, the longer Janine was unable to reach Toby the more frantic she became, knowing that Mary was slowly dying of dehydration at her hands. This morning she decided she had to act. She crept out of the hotel while George was still asleep, then caught the next available plane back to London.'

I stepped over to the window and surveyed the rather anonymous Hendon street. 'In fact, she could arrive any time now.'

Mo looked alarmed at the prospect. 'What do we do with her?'

'I haven't decided yet,' I replied thoughtfully. 'It depends on how she reacts to being rumbled. Mind you, I should have seen through her ploy considerably earlier than I did.'

'How?'

'Well, from the start I felt it was rather fishy that she fulfilled Beaumaris's requirements for the ideal woman *so* perfectly. You remember that conversation I had with her in the rose garden? I was questioning her about Top Table Introductions. She was being extremely unforthcoming – until I told her I might have to delve into the agency's files. Then she *suddenly* remembered that Toby had talked to a man in a pub about the figurines. I'm pretty sure, looking back, that that whole story was a concoction – a diversion – to make me forget all about researching into Top Table.'

Mo weighed this for a while. 'And Janine got her brother to back up her deception?'

'That's right.'

'One thing, though,' remarked my colleague, joining me at the window. 'You said Mary Catchpole was the woman Daphne and I saw – at the window?'

'Correct.'

'Why was she spying on us?'

'I imagine she was trying to intimidate Janine; to remind her that she had to keep paying up, or Beaumaris would learn about her fraud.'

'I see. And the veil?'

'Ah, that all started, I suggest, when Beaumaris turned up here, to Janine's flat. Mary Catchpole happened to be around at the time – conducting her blackmail. Obviously she couldn't allow Beaumaris to recognize her, so she hid her face and rushed into the bedroom. Beaumaris was curious to know who Janine's anti-social friend was. Janine had to think on her feet. She invented a shy muslim friend called Fatima, who was staying with her. It was so obscure that he believed it. From then on Mary decided to become Fatima and wear a veil whenever she visited Janine.'

'So there never was a schoolfriend with a scarred face? That was the whole basis of your first theory, wasn't it?'

'My first theory was completely wrong,' I admitted gracefully.

'Janine claimed it was all true, though,' pointed out Mo.

'Yes, to throw us off the scent; and at least it made her out to be altruistic, rather than simply scheming.'

Just then a mini-cab pulled up directly beneath us, and a figure wearing a wide purple hat emerged carrying a suit-case. We heard steps on the stairs and then a key turning in the lock.

Janine walked in, plonked the case on the floor, and rushed towards the bedroom without even noticing us.

'Good day, Miss Yorke!' I called after her cheerily.

She spun round, wild-eyed.

'You won't find Mary Catchpole in there – she's on her way to hospital. Don't worry, she'll probably be alright. But it was a near thing.'

Janine sank heavily into an armchair and then burst into tears of relief.

'You're lucky,' I added, once she had recovered and blown her nose. 'It could have been murder. Manslaughter at the very least. By the way, we know all about you working for Top Table, and that you were being blackmailed by Mary. We know everything in fact.'

'Have you told George yet?' she snivelled.

'No, not yet. He's waiting for my call, at the hotel. Perhaps it would be better if you talked to him yourself.'

'Why?'

'Don't you think you owe him that at least?'

She shrugged.

'Actually, I'm not sure of the legal situation, but he could claim that you married him under false pretences. In which case you lose the marriage settlement. As to Mary Catchpole, she may not press charges. It would mean admitting to the blackmail, wouldn't it?'

'But surely the police will want to know why she was left tied up,' observed Mo.

I thought about this. 'Mary could say she consented – that it was a bizarre game which went horribly wrong!'

Janine seemed to take some heart from the idea.

'I love George, you know,' she declared, looking almost defiantly at us. 'You may not believe me, but I do.'

'Frankly, what we think is neither here nor there,' I said, handing her the telephone. 'It's your husband who will need all the persuasion.'

THE BALCONY SCENE

CHAPTER ONE

It was just after five o'clock on a Friday afternoon in February, and we were about to put on our coats and close up the office for the weekend when an email came through. Business had been pretty slack recently so every new communication was given our promptest attention. I hurried over to the computer, and read it over a few times.

'Anything?' enquired Morris, hovering near the door with one arm in his anorak.

'I suppose it was only a matter of time,' I replied meditatively, 'before the Internet took over as the main medium for intimidation. How long after the invention of the telephone was the first obscene call made, do you think?'

'No idea. Who's the email from, anyway?'

'Kevin Tripp, managing director of X.E. Media Ltd. They publish "tasteful pornography", whatever that is. Apparently he's received an unusual death threat, on the Internet. Someone calling himself "Mad Monk" has visited the company's site and left a message warning that Tripp will be assassinated before the end of March.'

I handed the communication over to Mo.

'He obviously takes the threat seriously, judging by how much he's offering us up front,' remarked my colleague gleefully.

'I imagine it's easy to make enemies in the porn business,' I conjectured. 'Perhaps he has good reason to be frightened.'

'Did you read this bit? He wants us to go round to his office on Sunday to "receive instructions". Odd way of putting it.'

'Yes,' I agreed, 'that's exactly what I was thinking.'

The offices of X.E. Media turned out to be situated in a glass-and-concrete block in Capper Street, off Tottenham Court Road.

As it was Sunday the place was locked up, but we pressed the appropriate buzzer, and after a few minutes a short, tubby man of about forty appeared at the door and let us in.

'You're from Baskerville's, right?' he asked, looking us over with small, suspicious, close-set eyes.

'Indeed we are,' I replied breezily.

'This way,' he ordered.

Mo and I exchanged glances, unsure as to whether this was Tripp himself, or an underling.

We took the lift to the very top floor, and as it was a slow lift I had time to study our escort in detail. He wore a well-tailored double-breasted suit, a flowery silk tie, and highly polished brown brogues. But the expensive, executive image was somewhat undermined by his near-skinhead haircut. Also, I noticed a tattoo of a snake on his neck, which he was at pains to conceal by pulling up his collar. I attempted to make eye-contact with him on more than one occasion, but each time he averted his gaze, and sucked harder on his mint. His cheeks were excessively chubby, giving him the air of a slightly malign hamster.

Exiting the lift we made our way down a long, narrow corridor and into an office marked: K.TRIPP, MANAGING

DIRECTOR. Although comfortable, it was a little on the spartan side. Our attention was immediately drawn to a shelf running along the wall to our left upon which was displayed a bewildering array of girlie magazines.

'It's all harmless stuff, as you can see,' remarked the man blandly, following our gaze. He sat down behind the desk, drew out a packet of mints from a drawer, then popped one into his mouth, hardly before the last had been consumed. 'I wanted to have this meeting in private,' he explained. 'As you know, I'm in a dodgy situation. Somebody's trying to kill me.'

It was apparent from these last remarks that we were indeed addressing Kevin Tripp himself.

'We're nearly into March already,' he added, nervously looking across at a desk calender. 'This is the plan; I'm going to stay locked up in my house in Kensington for the whole month. I won't step outside the front door, not even to buy a newspaper. That way they'll have to take a potshot at me. Obviously I'll keep away from the windows as much as I can; the curtains will be drawn at all times. I won't let any strangers in, no matter who they are. Jack Earle – an old mate of mine – he's going to be my armed bodyguard. He'll be staying with me. I want you to work closely with him.'

'What will our role be, exactly?' I enquired.

'You'll be my eyes and ears, out on the street. Keep a look out for anyone acting suspicious, anyone taking an interest in the house. Also, find out who's living opposite and how long they've been there. It's a round-the-clock job, so you'll have to work out a shift system between yourselves. And I want a progress report every day. Any questions?'

I cleared my throat awkwardly, before commenting: 'To be frank, Mr. Tripp, this isn't the type of thing we normally undertake. Our expertise lies in deduction and analysis, rather than basic surveillance.'

'I'm paying you well over the odds, right?'

'Yes, I suppose you are.'

'For that money I expect you to do as you're told. There are plenty of other firms who'll take the work.'

Mo toyed with his adam's apple and gave me a kind of pleading look.

I bit my lip, and then answered: 'Alright, we accept your terms. But there's something I need to establish first.'

Tripp leant back in his chair, sucked hard on his mint, and allowed me a rare moment of sustained eye-contact. 'OK. What is it?'

'Have you any idea who this "Mad Monk" is?'

'No,' he answered quickly.

'Is that because you don't have any enemies, or because you have too many?'

Tripp's ferrety eyes narrowed, and he seemed about to react angrily. But the mood passed.

'Let me worry about that side of things, Mr. Webster. I've got my own methods. You just make sure you do your job properly.'

'Fair enough,' I agreed, with a shrug.

'OK, that's it for now,' announced our latest client, getting up and steering us towards the door. 'I want you to come round to my house on Tuesday, to get a feel for the area.' He scribbled a note on a scrap of paper and handed it to me. 'That's the address. And you can meet Jacko at the same time.'

'Your bodyguard?'

'Yes. He gets a bit out of order sometimes – but don't worry about it. I can trust him with my life.'

Tuesday came, and we taxied over to Tripp's house, which was an elegant, white, three-storey terrace in Oxshott Street, not far from South Kensington Tube.

'He's getting jittery already – the curtains are drawn,' observed Mo, scanning the building as we walked up to the well-maintained columned porch.

I rang the bell and the door was opened by a nondescript, grey-haired individual of about fifty who showed us into the reception room.

'Kevin won't be long,' he said, casting a weary eye up at the ceiling. 'He's having a barney with his girlfriend at the moment, I'm afraid.'

'Should we come back later?' asked Mo considerately.

'No, you may as well hang around until they finish. By the way, I'm Gordon, Kevin's older brother. You're here about the death threat, aren't you? Nasty business.'

I nodded. 'You take it seriously?'

'I don't know what to make of it, to be honest.'

'But your brother does have enemies?'

'Some people might call him ruthless,' he replied carefully. 'But that's how you've got to be in business. I've watched him build up the company from nothing, and I know exactly whose toes he's trodden on. I could make you a list, but I warn you it would be quite long.' He broke off to pour himself a glass of scotch. 'Want one?'

Mo and I both declined.

'I work for Kevin, did you know?' he continued conversationally. 'Yes, I'm his Finance Director – joined about five years ago. That's when profits started going through the roof. Kevin needed someone he could trust; someone from the family. Of course, my wife had scruples, but when she realized how much I was going to earn she forgot about them.'

'Scruples about the nature of the work?' I asked.

He nodded.

'At least you don't produce hard-core material,' put in Mo lightly.

A sardonic expression passed across Gordon's dull countenance. 'Is that what Kevin told you?'

'Yes.'

He looked up at the ceiling again, this time furtively. 'Well, if that's what he says, it must be true. Who am I to contradict the boss?'

'Then it isn't exclusively soft porn?' I asked.

Gordon took a copious slug of whisky and grimaced. 'No, we churn out all kinds of stuff. Some of it would make your hair curl. Actually, it's amazing how many different types of perversion there are. I'd never even heard of some –'

At this point he halted, and cocked an ear towards the door apprehensively. We could hear raised voices, one male and one female, then a door slamming. I wandered out into the hall in time to see a tearful, buxom brunette thundering down the stairs, carrying a large suit-case.

'I'll give you a ring tomorrow – promise,' called Kevin Tripp indulgently over the bannisters.

'Don't bother, you bastard!' screeched the girl. She walked straight past me as if I didn't exist, and out of the front door, without bothering to close it behind her.

'Sorry about that,' mumbled Tripp, descending rather sheepishly.

'Not at all,' I returned.

'I can't have her staying here while all this business is going on, can I? It's not safe. You'd think she'd jump at the chance of having a country house to herself.'

'Country house?'

'In the Cotswolds. I use it at weekends.'

At that point Mo came out of the reception room to see what was going on.

'Good, you're both here,' said Tripp. 'I'll introduce you to Jacko now. Follow me.'

We climbed the stairs and turned right into a large, dimly lit games room. There was a pool table in the centre, over which crouched a tall, athletically-built man with receding hair swept back into a tiny, neat ponytail. He potted a red ball, then looked up and gave us an unpleasant grin, revealing a chaotic set of teeth. He was wearing a holster containing some kind of handgun.

'Jacko, these are the people who are going to watch the house. If they see anybody hanging around they'll warn you.'

'And I'll be waiting for them,' added the henchman grimly, giving his gun an affectionate pat.

'Your shirt's hanging out at the back, mate. Sort it out, will you?'

Jacko obeyed, seemingly without resentment.

'I can't stand scruffiness,' explained Tripp, turning to me. 'It does my head in, you know.'

'Really?' I replied, looking at him slightly askance.

To me the criticism seemed ill-deserved because apart from the shirt Jacko's attire was immaculate – right down to the gold cuff-links and matching tie-pin.

'I've got to make a few calls,' said Tripp, 'so why don't you take a wander – have a look at the neighbourhood. There's a local map downstairs if you need it.'

'We've brought our own,' said Mo.

In fact our preparation had extended as far as researching all the properties in Oxshott Street. Of the twelve on the opposite side of the road none had changed hands in the past year, and none were being rented out, according to the available information. I therefore felt it unlikely that the assassin had taken up residence nearby. However, it was always possible that some unofficial sub-letting was going on.

'I'd like to take a look at your garden,' I requested. 'It would be useful to know how accessible the house is from that side.'

Tripp nodded and led us downstairs. When we reached the back door he paused.

'I'll stay inside, if you don't mind – I don't want to get sniped at.'

'It's not March until tomorrow,' Mo pointed out.

'Even so. I'll leave the door unlocked so you can get back in.'

We stepped out onto the rectangular lawn, which was still crisp with frost, and looked back at the house. A wrought-iron fire-escape spiralled up to the top floor, next to which nestled a satellite dish. The garden backed onto a huge, featureless brick building, which we already knew to be a municipal swimming pool.

'The assassin would have to come through these adjoining gardens, which would mean scaling a number of walls and fences,' I concluded, surveying the scene. 'Then he'd have to use the fire-escape and break in – perhaps through one of the windows.'

'It's possible,' said Mo.

'But difficult not to be seen. It would have to be a night-time assault.'

'You think we should concentrate on the front of the house, then?'

'On balance, yes. But really, the whole idea of wandering the length and breadth of South Kensington in search of suspicious characters is laughable – a complete waste of time. If Tripp wasn't paying us so much I'd tell him so to his face.'

'Aren't you being a bit defeatist?'

I shook my head. 'What we should be doing is investigating his enemies, in a systematic way. You know that as well as I do.'

'But he's adamant that we stick to our allotted task.'

'I know,' I replied with a frown. 'It's infuriating.'

My feelings of frustration mounted over the next three weeks, almost to the point where I was ready to chuck the whole thing in. It was Mo who kept me going, constantly reminding me of how healthy our bank balance was going to look by the end of the month.

We had developed a system of patrolling the surrounding streets, calling in at pubs and shops on our way. The shifts were long and the work repetitive. We made a note of any untoward happening or suspect individual. The information was condensed into a short bulletin and handed in to Tripp at the end of each day. He would then glance over it, make a few inconsequential comments, and throw it into the nearest bin. It was a ritual from which he appeared to derive some kind of peace of mind.

A little before seven one Saturday evening I arrived at the end of my tour of duty feeling particularly low. My feet ached, I was chilled to the bone, and I'd been accosted by a drunk. Mo met me at the end of Oxshott Street, and we headed for Tripp's house in search of a restorative cup of tea.

'Only a week to the end of the month,' said my associate, slapping me on the back encouragingly. 'No sign of any assassin. Do you think this Mad Monk thing could be a joke?'

'It's in pretty bad taste if it is,' I remarked sourly.

Just then there was a loud bang, as if someone had let off a firework nearby.

'What was that?' asked Mo, tugging at the sleeve of my overcoat.

'I don't know. Seemed to come from up ahead.'

We both accelerated into a run, and were within thirty yards of Tripp's place when a tall figure appeared on his balcony. Despite the fading light we were able to make out that it was someone dressed as a monk, with a cowl drawn up over their head. Suddenly the man pulled out a gun, waved it about, and screamed: 'Get down!'

The instruction was evidently aimed not at us, but at whoever was inside the house. Seconds later the odd apparition disappeared again through the balcony doors.

By now a few pedestrians had gathered alongside us on the pavement, anxiously gazing up at the unfolding drama.

'Is it a seige?' asked one lady.

'I think someone should call the police,' suggested a middle-aged gentleman authoritatively.

'You're right,' I said, getting out my mobile phone and dialling 999. While I was in the middle of explaining the situation to the female police operator there was a second loud report.

'Did you hear that?' I asked her.

'Yes, what was it?'

'Another shot. How soon can you get someone here?'

'It won't be long, sir. Don't approach the gunman under any circumstances.'

'He'll probably try to escape through the gardens at the back of Oxshott Street,' I predicted, 'so make sure you post some men there.'

'I'll pass that information on, sir.'

'Please do.'

I replaced the mobile in my coat pocket.

Mo asked: 'Do you think they'll act on your advice?'

'I wouldn't count on it.'

'What do we do until they arrive?'

'What do you suggest? I'm certainly not going to risk getting shot for Tripp's sake – are you? Let's just leave it to the professionals.'

Within an admirably short period a squad of police cars and an ambulance drew up at the end of the street. They were followed by an unmarked van which spewed forth a stream of armed officers, who immediately adopted various strategic positions within range of the house. The whole well-orchestrated process took no more than a couple of minutes.

'Right, I'll have to ask you all to move right back, please, right back,' said a constable advancing on us and waving his arms. 'We're clearing the street. Quick as you can, please.'

'I'm the person who rang you,' I informed him.

'Thank you, sir, but you'll have to move back for your own safety.'

We were herded like so many wayward sheep to a position from which we could only just see the balcony. I sought out the most senior-looking official I could find – who I later discovered to be Detective Inspector Poole – and apprised him of the likely personnel in the house.

'The owner is Kevin Tripp – a company director. There's also his bodyguard, Jack Earle, who carries a handgun. I'm rather afraid they've both been shot, Inspector – by the man dressed as a monk.'

'And you are?'

I showed the D.I. my card, which induced a raised eyebrow and an evanescent smile.

'Have you got the back garden covered?' I asked anxiously.

'Yes, of course we have.'

Just then the man in charge of the armed unit approached Poole, and took him off for a private discussion.

The unnatural silence which had recently descended upon Oxshott Street was eventually broken by the dramatic appearance of a short, plump woman. She flew out of Tripp's front door and ran down the pavement towards us, shrieking intermittently. I soon recognized her as Ruby Gates, Tripp's regular cleaning lady. She must have been in the house throughout the whole terrifying episode.

A couple of policewomen went forward to receive the poor thing, and helped her into the back seat of the nearest police car, where they offered what comfort they could. Poole joined them in the front seat. Once Ruby had recovered from the worst of her hysterics he began asking her questions, probably by way of a de-briefing.

I don't know what she told him, but it seemed to have a direct effect on tactics. Poole got out of the car and spoke into his radio, briefly. Within seconds the armed officers left their stations and began closing in on Tripp's house. They moved in little darting sprints, silently, almost balletically. Soon two or three had converged on the porch. At a given signal they stormed through the front door and out of sight.

Poole gazed intently at the balcony, exercising his jaw muscles, as the drama entered it's most critical stage. I was standing only a few feet away from him, so when the message was radioed through from the advance party I could hear every word. The news was not good; two men had been found in the house, both dead from gunshot wounds. From the brief descriptions it was clear that they were Tripp and Earle respectively. There was no sign of the killer.

CHAPTER TWO

Once Mo and I had given our formal statements at the local police station I requested a more informal interview with

Detective Inspector Poole. He took us into his office and closed the door.

'We'll be happy to assist you in whatever way we can,' I declared. 'As you know, my agency was hired to protect Kevin Tripp. Obviously we failed.'

'Obviously,' he smirked.

'However, if we'd been allowed to employ our usual methods things could have turned out differently.'

'Really?'

'Yes, I feel we might have been able to identify the killer before he struck. The least we can do now is help you track him down.'

Poole looked at me with amused scepticism. 'We've moved on a bit from Sherlock Holmes's day, you know. I don't see how you can compete with modern forensic techniques.'

'I can't. My approach is complementary.'

'And it works,' added Mo loyally. 'He's solved a number of cases already.'

Poole sank into his chair and rubbed his broad, badly-designed face thoughtfully. 'I'm not too proud to accept help from any source, if it gets a result. The big problem here is, what happened to the man dressed as a monk? He seems to have arrived at the scene and left again, without being spotted by anyone. Now that's quite a feat in a built-up area like Kensington. At least we know which direction he ran off in.'

'How do you know?' I asked.

'They found a monk's habit on the fire-escape. And the gun was lying on the lawn a few feet away. He must have run across the garden, jumped the wall, into the next garden, and so-on until he reached Warwick Mews. And he must have done it before we arrived. That suggests an athlete.'

'You don't have any witnesses at all?'

'No, none of the neighbours saw him.'

'But they can't have failed to hear the gunshots. Didn't that make them extra vigilant?'

Poole shrugged. 'It was getting rather dark, I suppose.'

'The gun you found – is that definitely the murder weapon?' asked Mo.

'It's been sent off to ballistics – but I'm confident it is. Both men were shot in the head, at close range.'

'Was there any sign of a struggle?' I asked.

'No, not really. Tripp was found in the main bedroom, face down on the carpet. Earle was in the hall – the revolver in his holster hadn't been fired.'

'Was there anything else of interest?'

'Needle tracks on Earle's arms – he was, or had been, a junky. Oh, and his polo-neck jumper was on inside-out – the label was showing.'

'What?' I exclaimed in surprise. 'Are you quite sure about that?'

'Yes. Why?'

'It's just that Kevin Tripp was absolutely obsessed about his employees being neat and tidy, wasn't he Mo?'

'Oh, definitely,' confirmed my friend.

'Well, I'm telling you, that's how we found him. Of course we should know a lot more about what happened when Ruby Gates gives us her account. She's likely to be our key witness.'

'How is she by the way?' I enquired. 'Still in shock?'

'Yes, but on the mend. I might visit the hospital tomorrow.'

'Would you mind if we came along? We got to know her pretty well while we were working for Tripp. She might relax a little if she sees a couple of familiar faces.'

'Alright. But I want something in return,' said Poole with a calculating expression.

'What's that?'

'This is going to be a high-profile case – what with the pornography angle, and the Mad Monk bit. So if we solve it between us, you let me get the credit. Fact is, I'm up for promotion later this year; I need all the brownie points I can get. Do we understand each other?'

'Of course, Inspector. We'll keep out of the limelight completely, just as Holmes himself did. You can be a kind of latter-day Lestrade if you want.'

'Yes, that's it,' said Poole, growing excited by the prospect.

Mo, on the other hand, looked distinctly underwhelmed. He was always in favour of publicity for Baskerville's at any cost. But the deal had been struck, for better or worse.

The following morning Poole telephoned to confirm that Mrs. Gates was now well enough to answer a few questions. He instructed us to meet him at the hospital in an hour.

We were there in good time, but the detective was half an hour late. He made no apology.

'You'll have to let me conduct the interview,' he said firmly, as we headed through the main concourse towards Ruby's ward. 'We've only got a limited time with her, and I want to extract as much information as possible.'

Having told the nurse behind the reception desk who we had come to visit we sat in the waiting area.

After a few minutes the Sister approached us and declared briskly: 'Mrs. Gates already has someone with her at the moment – I believe it's her son. But she'll see you. If you'd like to follow me.'

Kevin Tripp's unfortunate cleaning lady was sitting up in bed, drinking a cup of tea. A curly-haired young man in denims was seated close by, gazing at her with an expression of filial concern.

'Hello, Mrs. Gates. You remember me?' asked Poole.

'Yes, I do. They told me you were coming,' she replied, in her sing-song Welsh accent.

'I've brought Mr. Webster and Mr. Rennie along to see you.'

'You're going to ask me about the shooting, I suppose?'

'Only if you feel up to it.'

'I'll tell you what I can. Let's get this over and done with. Then you'll leave me alone, won't you?'

Poole smiled kindly. 'Of course we will.'

'This is my boy, Wyn.'

Wyn acknowledged us with a nod, then got up from his chair. 'I'd better be getting along now, Mam. I'll be back this evening, usual time. Don't let them tire you out.' He gave his mother a peck on the cheek and headed for the exit.

We settled down around the bed and waited for Ruby to finish her tea before telling her story.

'I was hoovering in the living room. Mr. Tripp and that Jacko character were upstairs. I heard the doorbell ring. Next thing I knew there was this tall man dressed like a monk, standing right behind me. It give me such a shock.'

'Did you see his face at all?' asked Poole.

'No, not really. It was covered with the hood. Anyhow, he grabbed me and put his hand over my mouth. Told me not to make a sound.'

'What was his voice like?'

'Calm, and soft. Cockney, I think.'

'Then what?'

'He pushed me out of the door, and shoved me into the cloakroom. Locked me in. After a while I heard the first shot.'

'From upstairs?'

'I'm not sure. There was a bit of shouting, then another shot. Then I heard footsteps. I thought he was coming back to get me. But he just unlocked the door and said: "It's over, I'm leaving." '

'Is that when you ran out of the house?'

'Oh no! I waited – to make absolutely sure he'd gone. I listened out for the sound of the front door, but I think he must have left by one of the back doors. Finally I plucked up the courage to come out of the cloakroom. And there was Jacko, lying in the hall in a pool of blood. I didn't stop to see whether he was alive, I got out of there as fast as my legs could carry me.'

The effort of recollection left Ruby looking drained; she sank back against her pillow and closed her eyes. This did not escape the attention of the Sister, who had been hovering nearby.

'I think that's probably enough for today, Ruby,' said Poole tactfully. 'You've been a great help.'

She answered with a weary nod, and we beat a respectful retreat.

'Disappointing,' muttered Poole, as we munched a spot of lunch in the hospital cafeteria. 'I thought we'd get a good description of the man's face, at the very least.'

'Give her time,' advised Mo wisely. 'As the shock wears off she'll probably remember everything more clearly.'

Poole appeared unconvinced. 'I can't hang around for that. There are questions to be answered. For example, if Tripp was so paranoid why did he let the monk into the house? Have you got any theories about that, Mr. Webster?'

I tried to imagine the likely sequence of events leading up to the murders. 'The killer rings the bell. Tripp speaks to him on the intercom, judges he isn't a threat, and lets him in. Perhaps he recognises the voice? Or he looks out of the window and sees that it's someone harmless – in which case the man couldn't have been wearing the monk's costume when he arrived.'

'You mean he changed into it when he got inside the door?' asked Mo.

'It's conceivable. But I grant you it would have to be an exceptionally rapid change, because he was in his habit by the time he grabbed Ruby – only a few seconds later.'

'At least that would explain why there are no witnesses to a monk arriving at the house,' said Poole. '*Somebody* in the vicinity should have noticed a conspicuous figure like that.'

'So, we should be looking for a tall man with a cockney accent, who was one of Tripp's trusted acquaintances,' summarised Mo.

'My money's on his brother, Gordon,' declared Poole, wolfing down his fifth sandwich. 'He doesn't have a satisfactory alibi. Claims he was walking around in Hyde Park – taking the air. But nobody saw him.'

'Does he have a motive, though?' asked Mo.

'According to my information Kevin's shares in the company pass straight to Gordon – which means he's now effectively in control. You can't get a better motive than that.'

'There are two objections to Gordon as a suspect,' I countered. 'First, he's not as tall as the man we saw on the balcony. Second, Ruby would surely have recognised his voice – she knows him well.'

'I still want to interview him again,' insisted Poole, 'if only to firm up his alibi. You're welcome to come along.'

Within the hour we were at the X.E. Media headquarters in Capper Street. Gordon, looking as drab and nondescript as ever, was in the process of moving into his brother's office – which seemed like indecent haste. The name-plate had already been changed.

'I don't really know why I'm bothering with all this,' he remarked, showing us in. 'I won't be here very long.'

'How's that, Mr. Tripp?' asked Poole suspiciously.

'I've decided to sell out – to one of our market rivals.'

'Really? That's quite a big decision to take, so soon after your brother's death.'

'I never cared for the business, to tell you the truth. I only joined because of Kevin, and now he's gone.'

'Who's the buyer?' asked Mo.

'Peter Van Meert. He owns a big Dutch media conglomerate. He's been after the company for months. Kevin dug his heels in and refused to sell. It became a kind of ego battle between them. But I can't be bothered with any of that sort of thing. Peter's prepared to pay a fair price – and I'll be able to retire.'

Assuming his more official tone, Poole said: 'I'm afraid I have to ask you to be more specific about your whereabouts at the time of the murders. You say you were strolling in Hyde Park. Surely there must have been some witnesses to that? What about one of the demonstrators?'

'Demonstrators?' echoed Gordon, looking blank.

'Yes, there was a huge rally of pensioners – protesting about the price of fuel. They were swarming all over Hyde Park at about the time you say you were there.'

Gordon shuffled the paperwork on his desk uncomfortably.

'Come on, Mr. Tripp. We may as well have the truth.'

'Alright, I suppose I'll have to take you into my confidence. No, I wasn't there. I was with a girl – in her flat.'

'I see,' replied Poole neutrally. 'Can we have the girl's name?'

'Is it necessary? Yes, of course it is. Her name is Tara Glover. She's one of our regular models. I've been seeing her on and off, ever since I started with the company. My wife doesn't know. It would kill her.'

'When did you arrive at the girl's flat?'

'About four. I didn't leave until after nine.'

'I presume she'll confirm this?'

'Of course she will.'

'And did anyone see you together? Think carefully – you've already given a false statement, remember.'

'We ordered a curry from a local take-away. The man who delivered it – he definitely saw me.'

'What time was this?'

'About seven-thirty, I think.'

'Where is the flat?'

'Windsor. The restaurant is called the Empress of India.'

'Fine,' said Poole, scribbling the details down in his notebook. 'We'll check up on all of this.'

'Try to be discreet,' entreated Gordon. 'My family means everything to me.'

'I'll do my best,' promised the detective with a nod.

'In return, I want to show you a list of my brother's enemies. I've been compiling it over the last week.' He took out a sheet of paper from a drawer and handed it over. 'All of these people had some kind of grudge against him and are capable of murder, in my opinion.'

'There are thirty names here, at least,' exclaimed Poole, looking rather shocked.

'All you have to do is line them up and get Ruby Gates to make an identification.'

'She didn't see the killer's face, though,' said Mo. 'We've just been talking to her in the hospital.'

'Pity. How is the old dear, by the way? I feel terrible about her getting mixed up in all this. Kevin always said she was the best cleaner he ever had. And the cheapest. You see that painting over there, leaning against the wall? I'm going to give it to her as a present – a kind of compensation. It's worth a few bob. British Impressionist, so they tell me.'

'It's very striking,' I commented, moving nearer to examine it. 'What's the scene? Cornwall?'

'No, the Gower Peninsula. That's where Ruby comes from. Trouble is, she's much too proud to accept it from me. I'm using her brother as a middle man. Actually he should be here by now – to pick it up. Hang on a minute.'

Gordon went out to have a quick word with his secretary in the next room, then returned.

'He's been waiting down in reception all the time. Can I call him up, or have you got some more questions?'

'No, go ahead,' said Poole, waving a permissive hand. 'We can tell him the latest about his sister's condition.'

A minute or so later a small, jovial looking man in his sixties with sparse, copper-coloured hair was shown into the office. Gordon directed him towards the painting.

'Well, Edwin, this is it. Tell your sister you bought it at a car-boot sale for twenty quid. You'll only be a thousand pounds out.'

'It's beautiful, Mr. Tripp!' Edwin enthused, holding it up to the light reverentially. 'I know she'll treasure it. I'll hang it up in her living room, ready for when she goes home.'

'Actually we've just come from the hospital,' remarked Poole. 'Ruby's doing well. The doctors are very pleased with her.'

'Yes, she's a tough old bird, my sister. Recovers quickly from any kind of adversity. Her daughter, Betty, died last year – heart failure. She took it so bravely. Mind you, she had to leave Wales because the memories were too painful. Moved up here to London. That was hard, because she loves the countryside.'

'Let's hope the painting cheers her up, then,' said Gordon kindly.

After a pause Poole announced: 'Well, I'd better be making tracks. We'll certainly analyse this list of yours, Mr. Tripp – see what our computer comes up with.'

'Let me know if it leads to anything, won't you?' I requested.

'Don't worry, I'll stay in touch,' promised Poole, as he wandered out.

Meanwhile Edwin had noticed the rack of porn magazines which adorned the wall behind us. He looked intrigued. 'So *this* is what your company does, Mr. Tripp. I had no idea.'

'Why don't you grab a few?' offered Gordon generously. 'We've got plenty of excess stock.'

'Well, I don't really know if I should.'

'Go on, don't be shy.'

'Alright, if you insist.'

Edwin moved along the display, picking out the odd magazine self-consciously. Then, as he neared the far end, he froze – with a curious, almost fearful expression on his face.

'Anything the matter?' asked Gordon, in a concerned tone.

'No, nothing,' replied Edwin, 'I'm not used to this kind of material, that's all.'

'Yes, some of it is a bit strong. Let's have the ones you've chosen. I'll wrap them up for you.'

Edwin handed over the pile, then sat down looking ashen-faced.

'Do you want me to wrap the painting as well?'

'No, I'll take it as it is.'

'Fair enough,' said Gordon, putting the magazines into a brown paper bag. 'Here you are, then.'

Edwin grabbed the bag in one hand and the picture in the other. 'I ought to go now. Ruby will be waiting. Thank you very much for everything.'

With that he made a hasty exit.

'Strange bloke,' commented Mo, gazing after him.

'Easily shocked,' I concluded.

Now that we were alone Gordon seemed anxious to talk about the police investigation, and his place in it. 'Does Poole really have me down as a suspect? You can be honest with me.'

'He did have,' I replied carefully, 'before you came up with a reasonable alibi.'

'As if I'd kill my own brother! It's ridiculous! Jacko – well, that's a different matter.'

'How do you mean?' asked Mo.

'Jacko deserved to get shot. He was a complete bastard. I don't know what Kevin used to see in him. Did you know he had form? The stories I could tell...'

'We'd like to hear them,' I encouraged.

'He used to choose the young, naive girls, and get them into drugs – coke and smack. Once they were hooked he forced them to do the really depraved stuff. He was a bloody animal.'

'And Kevin knew about all this?'

'Must have done – it was going on all around him. He thought Jacko was useful.'

'Did you ever voice your objections?' I asked.

Gordon looked ashamed. 'Not as often as I should. I didn't want to rock the boat. The money was too good.

But now you can understand why I want to get out of the business.'

Later that afternoon we went back to Oxshott Street, for the purpose of interviewing Kevin Tripp's neighbours about the murders. The police had, of course, done their own door-stepping, and drawn a complete blank. No-one had seen anything untoward, even though they may have heard the shots. But I felt it was worth double-checking.

Our efforts met with little success, until we rang on the bell of the house three doors down from Tripp's.

A nattily dressed elderly gentleman with a wonderful handle-bar moustache appeared.

'Yes? Can I help you?' he asked.

I lifted my deerstalker politely, and explained our business.

'Ah, so there *was* a murder!' he exclaimed.

'You didn't know?'

'I saw the police turn up, so I knew something odd was going on. But I couldn't hang around to find out more – my daughter was expecting me to meet her off a plane.'

'I see. So you haven't been interviewed by the police yet?'

'No, I only got back last night. I've been staying with her in Cheltenham.'

'In that case, may we possibly come in and ask you a few questions?'

'By all means,' said the old chap cheerfully.

He insisted on rustling up a spot of tea for us, during which he explained his version of the events of that fateful evening.

'I was watching a nature programme on the box when I heard the first bang. I went out into the back garden to see what it was. There was some shouting. Then came the second bang – definitely a gunshot this time. I was just about to go back inside to phone the police, when I spotted a dark, squarish object dropping out of a window.'

'Which window?' I asked excitedly.

'Third storey – three houses up the road from me.'

'What did it look like?'

'Just like a small parachute, really. It floated down onto the fire-escape.'

'Anything else?'

'No, I'm afraid not. I watched the window for some time – but that's all I saw.'

'You didn't spot a tall man running down that fire-escape, I suppose?' asked Mo.

'Oh no, nothing like that.'

'Are you quite sure? It was getting dark by then – perhaps you missed him?'

The man grew slightly irritated. 'My eyesight is still rather good, you know. Hasn't deteriorated since I was in the R.A.F. If there'd been someone there I would have seen him – but there wasn't.'

'Well, that didn't get us very far,' grumbled Mo, as we headed for the next house.

'On the contrary,' I replied, 'I think it's a very important eye-witness account.'

'But he didn't see anything!'

'Precisely. Just a dark object – presumably the monk's habit – dropping out of the window. But no sign of the monk. How do you explain that?'

'He must have already run off, I suppose.'

'But how could the habit float down like that of its own accord?'

'The wind blew it,' proposed Mo confidently.

'There was no wind that evening – not a breath.'

'What's your theory, then?'

'I haven't formed one yet. All I know is that there must be a fundamental flaw in the way we're imagining the sequence of events. Why did no-one notice the monk arrive or depart? Poole was quite right to be exercised by that question – I keep coming back to it myself.'

'Perhaps the killer was hiding in the house all the time? The police simply failed to find him.'

'But they turned the place over from top to bottom. It isn't that big a house.'

'What about a secret passage?'

I shook my head wearily. 'Now we're getting desperate…'

Having failed to gather anything more of interest from the remaining neighbours Mo suggested that we arrange an interview with Paulette, Kevin's girlfriend – the one whom we had seen being forcibly evacuated to the country. Surely she, argued Mo, would know what was going through his head during the last months of his life. I tended to agree, so we obtained her phone number from Gordon and gave her a ring. A flatmate answered, and informed us that she was on a late photo-shoot and would be back around nine.

We arrived at their Wembley flat at half-past nine. Paulette herself answered the door. We introduced ourselves and stated our business, and she reluctantly showed us into the lounge.

'I hope this won't take long – I'm knackered,' she warned, plunging onto the sofa as if it were a trampoline.

'Just a few questions,' promised Mo.

'I presume they haven't caught the bloke who did it.'

'No,' I admitted regretfully, 'we haven't caught him. Perhaps you can help to speed up the process.'

Paulette ran a hand through her back-combed brown locks and raised one of her exquisite eyebrows. 'How?'

'By telling us who Kevin was afraid of. Perhaps he had suspicions as to the identity of the Mad Monk?'

'If you're after bedroom secrets, forget it. Kevin didn't open up to me. He was a secretive little sod.'

Mo said: 'We've been given a list of his potential enemies by Gordon, but we need to be steered in the right direction.'

She let out an unladylike snort. 'Gordon gave you a list, eh? He should have put his own name at the top!'

'How do you mean?'

'He was always trying to go behind Kevin's back – making deals, fiddling the accounts. I never trusted him.'

'So it comes as no surprise to you that Gordon is selling the company to Peter Van Meert?'

'He was planning it for months. Kevin had to bug his office to find out what was going on. His own brother!'

'But is Gordon capable of murder, in your opinion?' asked Mo.

'I wouldn't put it past him. Or Van Meert. Have you investigated him yet?'

'No, he's based in Holland, and he's not on the list.'

I changed tack slightly. 'Tell us about Jacko. I understand he got some of the girls into drugs – is that correct?'

'Yes, it's correct,' she replied, in a subdued tone.

'But you weren't involved with him yourself?'

'I've got my head screwed on, unlike most of those bimbos. That's why I've ended up doing well-paid clothes modelling rather than the tacky work. Kevin introduced me to the right people. He didn't want any girlfriend of his flashing herself about. Talk about double standards!'

'Did you ever warn the other girls about Jacko?'

'Of course I did, all the time – they thought I was being an old hen.'

I took a bundle of girlie magazines from my coat pocket and spread them out on the coffee table.

Mo looked rather taken aback: 'Where did you get those, Sherl?'

'I swiped them off the shelf in Gordon's office. I didn't think he'd mind.'

Paulette gave me an old-fashioned look. 'So, you're a collector too, are you?'

'I just wanted to find out if these models are currently working for X.E. Media. Do you know this one, for example?'

She studied the cover carefully. 'That's Anna Smith. She dropped out of the scene some time ago.'

'Was she one of Jacko's girls?'

'I saw her hanging round him quite often, yes. Why are you asking?'

'Oh, just background research, really.'

She yawned. 'Well, if you don't mind, I'm crashing out now. Let me know if you find out who did it.'

At around lunchtime the following day Detective Inspector Poole turned up at the Crawford Street office looking particularly grave.

'More news from the Mad Monk,' he declared, refusing my offer of a beverage. 'I thought you'd want to hear straight away.'

'You mean there's been a sighting?' asked Mo.

'Worse than that. He's issued another threat – against Ruby Gates, this time.'

'What kind of a threat?' I enquired.

'She got a phone call from him this morning at her flat. He told her not to talk to the police any more, otherwise she'd end up like Kevin and Jacko – in the morgue.'

'Charming,' muttered Mo with a frown. 'This is all getting a bit out of hand, isn't it?'

'As you can imagine, I'm treating the matter extremely seriously. We've got a man posted outside the flat at the moment.'

'When did Ruby leave hospital, then?' I asked.

'She was released last night. Her son's staying with her until this business blows over – whenever that is.'

'What about her brother, Edwin?'

'I think she said he's gone back to his village in Wales. I've got the address somewhere.'

'I suppose Ruby is certain it's the same man who came into Tripp's house?' asked Mo thoughtfully.

'Yes, it was the same voice, and he called himself the Mad Monk. That name hasn't been released to the press yet.'

'Then he *knows* she's been talking to the police. How does he know?' I asked.

Poole shrugged. 'Perhaps he was spying on us in the hospital?'

'In which case,' Mo concluded deliberately, 'he'll have been picked up on their security cameras. I should study the video tapes carefully – look out for a tall man hanging around outside Ruby's ward on the day we talked to her.'

The detective sat stock-still in his chair, weighing Mo's advice carefully, before aiming a questioning glance at me. 'What do you think?'

'I think my colleague is perfectly right,' I replied.

'OK,' said Poole, jumping up with an air of decision. 'I'll request to see the tapes. Good idea, Mr. Rennie.'

Mo could not suppress a bashful grin.

'Before you go, Inspector, could you leave Edwin's address with me?' I requested.

'Yes. Why do you need it?'

'I want to go and see his house. It may be safer for Ruby to stay there – in a village setting – rather than in the town. Easier to protect her from the Monk.'

Poole nodded. 'Yes, I hadn't thought of that.'

After a quick bite to eat I drove over to my flat, packed a small suit-case, and then made for the M4. I had the entire length of that motorway to mull over the case, starting at Junction 1 in Gunnersbury, heading out of London, across Berkshire, Wiltshire, over the Severn Bridge, past Cardiff, and ending up at Junction 49, a few miles north of Llanelli.

By the time I finally reached Edwin's village it was just after eight o'clock in the evening. I had considered every likely hypothesis from a dozen different angles – rather like a chess player who calculates the permutations of an end game.

The house itself – a stone-built cottage – was easy enough to find, since there were only about twenty buildings in the entire hamlet. Edwin answered my knock and looked extremely surprised to see me.

'Don't be alarmed, I've just come to have a chat,' I explained quickly.

'Has anything happened to Ruby?' he demanded.

'No, she's fine.'

'Oh. Well, you'd better come in anyway.'

Still somewhat bemused by my presence he ushered me through into the cosy low-ceilinged dining room, where his wife was laying the table. 'This is Mr. Webster, dear, the man who's investigating the murders. My wife, Meg.'

'Will you join us for a bit of supper?' she asked hospitably. 'There's plenty here. You must have had a long journey.'

'Thank you, that's very kind.'

As we settled down to the stew Edwin gave me a searching look. 'So, what did you want to discuss exactly?'

I explained about the threat that Ruby had received earlier that day from the Mad Monk.

The news had a strange effect on Edwin. The edges of his mouth curled up very slightly, almost against his will, and his eyes shone brightly. If I didn't know better I would have said he was relieved.

By contrast, Meg tutted and shook her head sadly. 'What that poor woman has had to put up with! Is there anything we can do to help?'

'Well, as a matter of fact there is something,' I replied. 'She needs a safe place to stay for a while, and I wondered whether you could possibly put her up? We'd arrange full police protection, of course, until the Monk is caught.'

'There is a spare bedroom – not very big, though,' said Edwin doubtfully. 'What do you say, Meg?'

'Ruby's welcome to it, of course. It's the least we can do. Especially as her old house is being let.'

'What old house?' I asked.

'The family used to live near Bishopston, on the coast. When she moved away to London she let the house out to holidaymakers.'

'I suppose that was after her daughter, Betty, died?'

Meg nodded. 'That's right. Such a beautiful girl, Betty was.'

'Have you got a photo of her?' I asked casually.

'No, I'm afraid we haven't,' replied Edwin positively.

Meg was not so sure. 'Perhaps there's one in the bedroom. I'll go up and see.'

'Don't bother. I've just remembered: Ruby gave me one a few days ago,' I said, untruthfully. 'Here it is.'

I produced a shot of a girl's face, which I'd carefully snipped out of one of the X.E. magazines. 'That's her, isn't it?'

Meg nodded, and repeated: 'Such a lovely girl.'

'She died of heart failure, I understand? Was it sudden?'

'Well, to be honest she had been looking rather ill for some time before, hadn't she Edwin? I always said London didn't agree with her.'

'She was in London?'

'Yes, worked as a secretary there for two or three years. Then she came back, and a few weeks later we heard she was dead.'

Edwin mumbled a response. He seemed uneasy about discussing the subject.

After the meal we had coffee. Meg asked me where I was planning to spend the night, and I mentioned a pub which I'd seen up the road. She wouldn't hear of such an idea, and insisted that I stay with them.

The following morning I woke early, packed my suit-case, and left, but not without first having a useful natter with Meg. I winkled out of her the name of Ruby's family G.P. – a Dr. Branscombe. He still practiced in the Bishopston area, apparently.

The weather was unpleasant and squally, but the drive down to the Gower coast was spectacular, nonetheless. I stopped the car several times to take in the view, like an out-of-season tourist, and even went so far as to take a short walk along a cliff-top path. Thus invigorated I made my way to Dr. Branscombe's surgery, which was in the heart of Bishopston. He agreed to see me, briefly, between patients.

'I'll be as direct as possible, doctor,' I began. 'You were Betty Gates's G.P.?'

'Yes, that's correct.'

'I'm investigating a double murder in London, in collaboration with Detective Inspector Poole of the Metropolitan Police. Could you tell me what Betty died of?'

'I'm not sure that I can discuss that with you.'

'Well, can't you at least tell me what's written on the death certificate? That's surely a matter of public record.'

'Very well,' said Branscombe after a pause. 'She died of a heroin overdose.'

'Suicide?'

'Accidental, as far as we can tell. May I ask how this relates to your murder enquiry?'

'It may not relate to it,' I replied. 'But your information has been invaluable. I won't take up any more of your time.'

I left the doctor looking rather confused, and headed out of the surgery.

Just then my mobile rang. It was Poole.

'We're thinking of charging someone,' he announced abruptly. 'I thought you ought to know.'

'Charging someone? Who is it?'

'Shaun Woodruff – one of the names on our list. He and Kevin ran a strip club together in 2003. Kevin conned him out of several grand. We also found out he spent three month's in a Buddhist monastery when he was in his twenties.'

'Is that it?' I reacted, somewhat dismissively.

'No. We arranged for Ruby to come to the station and listen to Woodruff's voice. She positively identifies him as the same man who telephoned her this morning. I think you'd better get back here.'

'Yes,' I agreed, 'I'll start immediately.'

CHAPTER THREE

Several wearisome hours later I arrived at the police station to be met by an exuberant Poole. His normal, down-in-the-mouth expression was replaced by a smiling, sunny countenance. To be honest, I hardly recognised him.

'There could be a confession any time now,' he declared, leading me upstairs to his office with a boyish skip in his step. 'I've got a good feeling about this one.'

'You're still relying on Ruby's identification of Woodruff's voice?'

'Yes, and his history. He tried to get Kevin Tripp done over by a gang in a Deptford pub. Luckily Kevin was tipped off just in time and managed to escape; but they were ready to break his legs – or worse.'

'When was this?'

'Nearly seven years ago.'

'And Woodruff has waited all this time before having another go?'

'The circumstances had to be just right.'

'How tall is he?'

'Over six foot.'

'And I presume he doesn't have an alibi?'

'Paper thin. We'll be able to break it within twenty four hours,' predicted the detective confidently. 'We've got our forensic team looking over his house at the moment. And then there's the link with monks – don't forget that.'

'Oh yes. How long was he in this monastery?'

'Only a few weeks – but that's enough time to give him the idea of the name.'

'Quite.' I paused a moment to weigh up all this accumulated evidence before asking: 'What about Gordon Tripp's alibi? Did that check out in the end?'

'Yes, the delivery man from the Indian restaurant remembers seeing him in the girl's flat. I think we can safely eliminate him.'

'And the other names on that list?'

'There are several interesting leads that we haven't had time to pursue, in case Woodruff turns out to be innocent. But I think he's guilty. By the way, what happened in Wales? Is Ruby's brother willing to put her up?'

'He is, yes.'

'Good. I'm sure it's a good idea – even if we charge Woodruff. She needs to get as far away as possible, for the sake of her nerves.'

'Well, let me know if your man does confess,' I said, heading back down the corridor.

'Where are you going?'

'I ought to get back to Crawford Street. And then I might call in on Ruby.'

Mo was fast asleep on the sofa when I arrived at our office. A gentle nudge was enough to wake him, however.

'Oh, you're back,' he observed, yawning. 'What time is it?'

'Just after seven. Has everything been quiet here?'

'As a grave. Poole rang. He's got someone in custody – a prime suspect, apparently.'

'I know. I called in at the station on my way.'

'What do you think?'

'About Woodruff? I've got an open mind.'

'That new witness has put a spanner in the works, though.'

'What do you mean?' I asked, looking blank.

'Didn't Poole tell you? There was a builder doing a conversion job on the house opposite Tripp's. He had a clear view of everyone coming and going in the street.'

'And?' I asked impatiently.

'He came forward this morning, to say he didn't see a monk arriving. In fact he swears that *no-one* came in or out of Tripp's door for at least three hours before the murders took place.'

'But he saw the monk appear on the balcony, I presume?'

'Oh yes, he saw that alright.'

'Excellent!' I cried, punching the air with my fists.

'Why is it excellent?'

'Because it confirms that there's a deep fault-line running through the case, as I've always maintained. No wonder Poole neglected to tell me. He desperately wants everything to be straightforward.'

Feeling buoyed by the news I made Mo a cup of coffee and waited for him to wake up a little. Then we both drove over to Ruby's flat in Shepherd's Bush. On the way I rehearsed the formidable difficulties attending the case, as much for my own benefit as for my associate's.

'A murderer who appears and disappears from the scene of the crime as if by magic – by quantum leaps. That's the grotesque scenario we're faced with. But we *must* face it, otherwise we're simply running away from the evidence.'

'Like Poole is doing?'

I nodded. 'It seems a trifle premature to go around trying to elicit confessions from people, when you still haven't the faintest idea how the murders took place. That's not to say we don't have clues. Take Jacko's inside-out sweater. Could that not be a highly significant item?'

'I don't follow you,' confessed Mo.

'Well, we know that Kevin Tripp expected impeccable tidiness from employees. Jacko would never normally have dared to walk around with a label sticking out. Which suggests several interesting hypotheses.'

Mo shook his head rather sadly. 'I still don't see what you're driving at.'

I passed swiftly on to the subject of Ruby's daughter, Betty. 'Did you know she died of a heroin overdose? And she did some nude modelling for X.E. magazines?'

Mo looked shocked. 'Are you sure?'

'Absolutely. I confirmed both facts when I was in Wales.'

'Do we have to tell Ruby? It would devastate her if she found out.'

'Perhaps there won't be any need to tell her…'

A few minutes later we turned into a quiet residential street near Shepherd's Bush Green, and secured a rare parking space. A short stroll brought us to Ruby's address. When we rang the bell the curly-haired head of Wyn appeared fleetingly at a first floor window.

Eventually he opened the door to us and declared: 'Mam's out shopping at the moment.'

'Ah, I see. When will she be back?' I enquired.

'Not long. Half an hour perhaps.'

'Could we come in and wait?'

Wyn seemed hesitant. 'I suppose – if you want.'

We followed him up the stairs into the flat, which was tidy, though hardly spacious. Gordon's painting of the Gower coast was already hanging on the wall, proudly positioned above the mantelpiece.

I noticed that there was a complete absence of photographs, which prompted me to ask: 'Are there any family snaps lying about the place, Wyn?'

He looked surprised by the question. 'Why do you want to know?'

'I just wondered if you have a picture of your sister, Betty.'

'She's dead,' replied the lad simply.

'Yes, I know that.'

After this inconclusive exchange the conversation all but dried up. There was an awkward wait of ten minutes or so before Ruby arrived.

Although startled by our presence she seemed pleased enough to see us. 'It's kind of you both to drop by.'

'Not at all,' I returned. 'I just wanted to tell you that I've been down to Wales today, to see your brother.'

'Yes, he phoned me just after you left. Thanks for your concern, but I don't need to stay with him now. They've caught the Mad Monk, so I'll be quite safe. I've already sent the policeman away.'

'The policeman who was protecting you?'

'Yes. Mind you, I think he's still hanging around in the street.' She went to the window and parted the curtains. 'There he his, sitting in that car. It's a waste of resources, really. There's no danger any more.'

'But what if Woodruff isn't the murderer?'

'He's the murderer alright. It's the voice that gave him away. I'll remember it till the day I die. So calm, and yet cruel at the same time.'

'Would you be prepared to testify against him?' asked Mo.

'I would,' she replied emphatically, drawing herself up to her full height. 'Whatever the danger.'

'You're a brave lady,' said my colleague admiringly.

'Not really. It's my duty, isn't it, Mr. Webster?'

I shrugged. 'Well, it certainly takes guts to do what you've done. Also a good deal of planning, and an imaginative flair. I see from your shelf that you enjoy a good detective novel.'

'Yes, I read them occasionally,' answered Ruby, looking puzzled at my line of conversation.

'I thought so. You see, in my humble opinion Kevin Tripp and Jacko Earle were murdered by someone well versed in elaborate plots – just like yourself, in fact.'

An uncomprehending hush descended. Mo glanced at me with a frown. 'What are you saying, Sherl?'

'I suppose in my clumsy, roundabout manner I'm accusing Ruby of committing the murders.'

The words jolted my colleague like a cattle-prod. 'What!'

'Yes,' I went on languidly, 'she shot both Kevin and Jacko in cold blood.'

'What are you on about?' demanded Wyn, putting an arm around his mother's shoulders and giving me a menacing stare. 'You ought to watch what you're saying! She's just come out of hospital.'

'Shall I justify my statement by reconstructing the chain of events?'

'Yes, I think you'd better,' urged Mo, who seemed convinced I was making a catastrophic blunder.

I directed my remarks at Ruby herself.

'Your daughter, Betty, came to London a couple of years ago to work as a secretary. Being extremely pretty – and naive – she was an easy target for exploitation. Someone persuaded her to try glamour modelling for X.E. Media, as a quick way to make extra cash. At first things went well. But then she fell in with Jacko Earle. He got her hooked on heroin, which inevitably resulted in her having to do more and more hard-core material to feed her addiction. By the time she went back to Wales she had spiralled down into a state of self-loathing despair.

'As a caring mother you couldn't help but notice how run-down she appeared, and quizzed her about what she had been doing. In the end the whole sordid truth came out. A few weeks later Betty took the fatal overdose: either by accident, or by intent. To protect her reputation you told your brother, Edwin, that she had died of heart failure.

'Now you decided to wreak revenge on the two people who had contributed most to her death – Kevin Tripp and Jacko Earle. You insinuated yourself into Tripp's house by becoming his regular char. Then you sent him that Mad Monk message on the Internet, no doubt with Wyn's help. I believe that your son was originally going to be the assassin, dressed in the monk's habit. But then Tripp happened to invite Jacko to become his live-in bodyguard. Here was an unmissable opportunity to kill too despicable birds with one stone.

'On the afternoon in question you arrived at Tripp's house as normal, ready to carry out your duties. But there were two additional items in your cleaning bag: a revolver, and a monk's costume. Timing was important. You wanted Mr. Rennie and myself to witness the little drama which was about to be played out. So you waited until the end of my tour of surveillance before making the first move.

'You took the gun out of the bag, went into Tripp's bedroom, and shot him at close range. It was simplicity itself, because you were the very last person he feared. When Jacko heard the noise he hurried up to see what was going on. When he came into the room you put your gun to his head and threatened to shoot him too, unless he did exactly as he was told.

'You made him hand over his weapon, strip off, and put on the monk's robe. Then, on your signal he was to burst out onto the balcony, wave his now unloaded gun in the air, and shout "Get down!" We witnessed that performance, and it was undoubtedly thoroughly convincing. Finally you ordered him to change back into his normal attire, whereupon you shot him.

'The monk's habit and the gun you flung out of a back window; they landed on the fire-escape and lawn respectively. Having waited for a suitable crowd to assemble outside you then rushed out of the front door screaming hysterically. There – have I missed anything out?'

Ruby, who had been shaking her head almost continuously throughout my statement, now let out a sigh. 'What can I say? You're wrong.'

'What a pity – for a moment I thought you were about to make a confession. Oh well!'

'Does Inspector Poole go along with your theory?' she asked challengingly.

I smiled. 'I haven't actually put it to him yet. But no doubt he'll come round to my view – in the end.'

What happened next was as unexpected as it was violent. Wyn, who had contrived to walk round behind us, picked up a glass ornament shaped like a swan, and brought it down on Mo's head with considerable force. The object smashed into pieces, and my friend slumped to the floor. Then, before I had time to react, a long-bladed pen-knife was held to my throat.

'Don't, Wyn!' exclaimed Ruby, rushing forward to intervene.

'Why not?' he shouted. 'They haven't told the police yet, have they? We'll say the Monk killed them! Alright?'

'I don't know,' said Ruby, wringing her hands in indecision.

I tried to break loose, but Wyn was stronger than his slight physique suggested.

'There's no proof!' I panted 'You're safe!'

'Let him speak,' said Ruby. 'I want to hear what he has to say.'

Wyn eased his grip a fraction.

'You'll get away with it,' I continued. 'That's what I was going to tell you, but you didn't let me finish.'

Ruby nodded. 'He's right, Wyn, they don't have any proof. Come on, let him go.'

She tried to pull the knife out of her son's hand, and in the struggle the central lampshade was knocked. That must have alerted the policeman who was watching the house, because in a few seconds there was a prolonged ring on the doorbell. Realizing the position was fast becoming hopeless Wyn threw me aside.

'Alright, Mam, what the hell do we do now?' he asked breathlessly.

Ruby paced up and down the room, trying to determine the best course of action.

'Let the policeman in, ' she said at last. 'I'll tell him you lost your temper because they were making false accusations against me. Go on, boy– quick!'

Wyn hurried out of the door obediently. Meanwhile I attended to Mo, who had just come to and was groaning. I saw that there was a nasty looking gash on the side of his head – it was bleeding profusely.

'He needs to get to a hospital,' said Ruby. 'I'll phone an ambulance for you.'

'No need,' I retorted, glaring angrily at her. 'The policeman will do it.'

Two days later I called in at Mo's flat in Fulham. He had only recently been allowed home, and his head was still heavily swathed in bandages, producing a lop-sided turban effect.

'I've got to go back in a week or so, to have the stitches removed,' he remarked, showing me into the living room. 'And they want to do a few more tests on my brain.'

'This is all my fault, I'm afraid,' I mumbled guiltily. 'I should have known Wyn would do something desperate under pressure.'

Mo shook his head gingerly. 'He obviously panicked – difficult to predict that. But you might have told me your suspicions about Ruby before we went into the house.'

'Yes, I was doing my usual Holmes trick of keeping you in the dark until the last moment. Childish, really.'

'Your father would have approved.'

I laughed. 'Oh yes, I'm sure he would. Funnily enough, I was just thinking about him on the way over here.'

'Really? What about him?'

'All those wasted years when we never talked to each other – just because I resented my middle name. And now look at me.'

'One of life's little ironies – or big ironies,' Mo commented with a chuckle.

'Well, presumably you want to hear the latest?' I said, taking a seat. 'They've arrested Ruby and Wyn Gates, but it's likely the C.P.S. will throw out the murder charge.'

'The case is too hypothetical, I suppose?'

'I'm afraid so. If a link was found between either one of them and the murder weapon – that would be another matter. At least Wyn will go down for his assault on us.'

'That's something,' reacted Mo with a sniff. 'What about Poole? Does he accept Ruby's the killer, or is he still hanging onto Woodruff?'

'No, I've convinced him it was Ruby – for what it's worth. He even wanted to know how I first arrived at my conclusion. I gave him a little lecture in his office, while he took notes. It was most amusing.'

'And how *did* you arrive at your conclusion, if I may ask?'

'I'll tell you another day – you should be resting your brain.'

Mo made a face. 'I've done enough of that – I'm yearning for stimulation. At least tell me when you began to suspect Ruby.'

'Quite late in the day,' I admitted. 'Initially it was more a case of being vaguely unhappy with the behaviour of the monk. That appearance on the balcony seemed unduly melodramatic – the timing too convenient…

'You remember when Edwin had his funny turn – while he was choosing the porn magazines? That was really the crucial moment for me. I could tell from his face that he had recognised someone he knew – a close friend or family member. What else would produce such a look of shock? I thought it might well be Betty he had seen, because she was the right age, and described as beautiful. It occurred to me that if her untimely death had been in some way connected to her modelling it would give Ruby an excellent motive for killing Tripp – the owner of the magazines.'

'And she certainly had the opportunity – she was right on the scene.'

'Precisely. Both factors together made quite a compelling argument for suspecting her. Edwin had the same thought when he saw Betty's photograph. Realizing his sister could be a double-murderess was something of a jolt to the system.'

'No wonder the poor guy had to sit down,' Mo commiserated.

'Luckily I'd noticed which magazines he was looking at when he reacted so strongly; I managed to sneak them out with me. It was quite easy to ascertain which model was Betty, because she had a marked resemblance to her mother – especially in the mouth. Paulette's information merely confirmed the fact – although she knew Betty by an alias, Anna Smith.'

'Then you went to Wales on the pretext of finding Ruby a safe-house,' recalled Mo, 'and discovered that Betty died of a heroin overdose.'

'Yes, Jacko had obviously got her hooked. Ruby's motive for killing him and Tripp was now beyond doubt. But I still didn't know *how* she'd committed the murders. I thought of Jacko's inside-out sweater. He must have taken it off at some point, and then put it back on in a tremendous hurry. He was also roughly the same height and build as the man on the balcony. I began to suspect that Ruby had forced him to change into the habit and act out that scene – at gunpoint. It was really the only possible way to explain why no-one saw a monk arrive or depart.'

'And Ruby made up the story about being threatened on the phone – to divert suspicion away from herself?'

'And to ensure that we continued to believe in the existence of the Mad Monk character.'

Mo rubbed his bandaged head thoughtfully. 'She seemed such an ordinary sort of woman, that's the terrible thing.'

I shrugged. 'Her beloved daughter had been corrupted and driven to an early grave. The urge for revenge transformed her into a cunning killer. She leased out her house in Wales and rented a small flat in Shepherd's Bush instead – just so as to be near her intended victim.'

'That was a clue in itself.'

'With hindsight, yes.'

'One criticism. Wouldn't it have been better to wait until you had definite proof before confronting Ruby?'

'It was a fine judgement to make, Mo. I wasn't particularly sanguine about the prospects of obtaining a watertight case. There was a chance, however, that Ruby could be shocked into a confession. As it happened it was Wyn who lost his nerve, with evil consequences for you, I'm afraid.'

'We're in a hazardous profession,' he responded generously. 'At least we got a good fee, and an entertaining case.'

'I must say, the whole Monk stratagem was undeniably elegant,' I agreed. 'It gave Ruby something far better than an alibi – it gave her a legitimate reason for being at the scene of the crime.'

'You sound as if you admire her, Sherl.'

'If it wasn't for the fact that she tried to frame Shaun Woodruff for the murders I might admire her. After all, Tripp and Earle were hardly pillars of the community. What does Bacon say? "Revenge is a kind of wild justice."'

'Talking of bacon,' said Mo, 'I haven't eaten since breakfast. Shall we knock something up?'

'How about the Greek place down the road?'

'Looking like this?' he objected, pointing to his head.

'Why not? I'll wear my topper. We'll both be as conspicuous as each other, for once.'

9 781786 080509